COLONY ONE MARS

A SCIENCE FICTION THRILLER

GERALD M. KILBY

OUTER PLANET
MEDIA

For notifications on promotions and updates for upcoming books, please join my Readers Group at www.geraldmkilby.com.
You will also find a link to download my technothriller REACTION and the follow-up novella EXTRACTION for FREE.

CONTENTS

PROLOGUE

hat follows is the last known communication from Colony One Mars:

Sol #1:435 COM ID:N.L-1027.

This may be our last transmit for some time, we cannot spare the power. Sandstorm continues unabated, it will never end. We are down to 17% energy levels and have deactivated all non-essential systems. Solar array unable to recharge batteries due to darkened sky, running at only 7% efficiency. Plutonium power source has failed and attempts by EVA to find the fault have proved fatal. Those who have ventured outside to investigate have not returned. If the storm does not clear we will run out of power in approximately fourteen sols.

To add to our woes, a strange malaise has overcome many of us who still survive. A disturbing psychosis now affects one in three. We are prepared as best we can. We all know what is coming. We wait in hope, even though that now seems futile. Send no more.

1

DESCENT

In less than fifteen minutes Dr. Jann Malbec would be either walking on the surface of Mars or be dead, and there were plenty of ways for her to die. She could burn up in the atmosphere if the heat shield failed or be smashed to pieces on the surface if the thrusters didn't fire. In any event, it was going to be one hell of a ride.

After months of floating around inside the Odyssey transit craft en route to Mars, the moment had finally arrived for the six crew of the International Space Agency (ISA) to enter the lander and descend to the planet's surface. The habitation module was already in situ along with a myriad of equipment and supplies. The mothership would now be parked in orbit where it would wait patiently for their return.

Jann strapped herself into the seat, gripped the metal armrests tightly and tried to breathe normally. Ahead of her, at the flight controls, Commander Robert Decker and First Officer Annis Romanov cycled through the systems check routines.

"Detaching in five... four... three..." The voice of the first officer squawked in Jann's helmet and she felt a thud behind her as release bolts retracted. The lander detached itself, floating free from the mothership. A moment later thrusters fired to align it for the correct injection trajectory. Jann felt the force propelling her forward. Her grip tightened on the armrest. It bit through her gloved hand; it comforted her.

Gravity began to tug at the craft as it commenced its downward spiral. It shook. Gently at first. But with each passing second the vibration intensified and deepened until the entire vessel rocked with a violent cacophonous rage. The first officer began to shout out the descent velocity and elevation vectors.

"Mach two point seven. Altitude fifteen point six kilometers."

Jann tried not to think about the searing temperature building up on the craft's heat shield as it ploughed through the upper atmosphere. She gripped the armrest tighter and hung on.

It should have been Science Officer Patty Macallester sitting in this seat instead of her. But four weeks before the launch, Macallester started feeling unwell. An examination by the ISA medical team quickly diagnosed a viral infection. Not life threatening, but she would not be fit for the mission.

So, after much deliberation and hand wringing by the ISA directorate, Dr. Jann Malbec got the call. She was officially next in line and checked most of the boxes for most of the stakeholders but she was least experienced in terms of astronaut training. Jann knew the journey here was the easy part. The real test was beginning now. She would soon find out if she had what it took, or if she was simply an impostor.

The craft accelerated through the thin upper atmosphere and Jann felt a sickening wave ripple through her gut as her stomach began to form a closer relationship with her throat. The staccato voice of the first officer echoed in her headset as she checked off stats. "Mach one point seven, altitude ten point one, lateral drift two point two. Get ready, deploying chutes..."

With that, three enormous chutes exploded from the top of the descent craft and the vessel slowed down dramatically. Jann felt like she was being vacuum packed into her seat as they all took heavy G, as they hurtled towards the surface at extreme velocity. The thin Martian atmosphere—only 1% of Earth's—was grossly insufficient to slow the craft down for a soft parachute landing. At best it took just enough sting out of the free fall to engage the retro-thrusters.

"Detaching heat shield in three... two... one..." Jann felt the thump of bolts as the shield fell away from the base of the craft to find its own way down to the surface.

"Prepare for chute jettison..."

For a brief moment Jann's stomach resumed its

relationship with her throat before she was vacuum packed to the seat again.

"Retro-thrusters engaged... one point eight kilometers... targeting on HAB beacon... lateral drift still at two point two." The first officer and commander traded data, ticking off the distance to the surface and speed of descent.

"One point six... one point one... drifting..."

Slowly Jann's body resumed some ability to move and she shifted in her seat to reassure herself that she could still do it.

"Five hundred... three fifty... two seven five... hold on to your butts... here we go..."

The craft thumped down onto the planet surface. Landing gear took the strain and there was a brief moment when the stanchions held the full force before springing back to a complete rest. The thrusters shut off, the noise stopped and the craft was silent.

Stillness permeated the interior as the crew adjusted to the realization that they had landed, and that they were all still alive.

"Holy crap," it was the Chief Engineer, Kevin Novack, who broke the moment. Then followed a multitude of cheers and hand slapping. There was a palpable air of excitement mixed with intense relief that they had all survived the ride of death.

"It looks like we're about one klick from the HAB beacon." The commander pointed to a flashing blip on the main screen. " If our calculations are correct then the sandstorm should be about five kilometers west of us. Plenty of time to reach the Habitation Module."

They had been tracking the storm for some time while still on board the Odyssey. After much deliberation with ISA Mission Control it was decided to land now before the storm had chance to grow. If left too long it could engulf the entire area, making descent too risky and mean waiting weeks in orbit for another window.

It was a sandstorm that proved the undoing of Colony One, the first human settlement on Mars. It raged for over six months during which time all contact was lost. That was three and a half years ago. The crew of the ISA Odyssey was here to find out what had happened to it—and the fifty-four people who had called it home.

Annis ran through the lander shutdown sequence, flicking off switches and putting the craft into sleep mode. When the time came to return to Earth, it would be woken up, refueled from the methane/oxygen plant already on the surface and prepped for reuse as the Mars ascent vehicle (MAV) to rendezvous with the Odyssey orbiter.

"Prep for pressure equalization."

A chorus of '*check*' echoed in Jann's helmet as each crewmember confirmed the integrity of their EVA suit. Jann lifted her arm to adjust her helmet. It felt like lead. After so much time spent in zero gravity her body struggled to adjust to a new way of working. She managed to activate the heads-up display that gave her a status on vitals: pressure, oxygen, temperature and a raft of other biometric data. The others were also moving very slowly, readjusting to the one-third gravity.

"Okay, let's do this." The commander unfastened himself from his seat, opened the door to the Martian atmosphere and headed outside. In a well-practiced routine they followed in turn. Jann was last to leave. She felt totally uncoordinated as her body tried to remember how to move without floating. She clambered out backwards through the small hatch and fumbled to find the foothold that should be there—somewhere.

"See that on the horizon? It doesn't look good," said Annis.

"Damn, I thought we had calculated it was moving north of us." The commander was agitated. "Malbec, hurry up. We've got that storm heading our way."

"Sorry, Commander, can't find the foothold."

"Good God, would somebody please help her."

She felt a hand on her boot and her foot was guided to the rung. She scrambled down, stumbled on the final step and ended up facedown on the surface. She felt like she was glued to the dirt. *Gravity's a bitch*, she thought.

"Come on Malbec, move it." Decker was getting impatient.

Jann sat up, and with the help of Medical Officer Dr. Paolio Corelli and Mission Seismologist, Lu Chan, she was bundled upright.

"Thanks," she managed.

They were in the Jezero Crater, a forty kilometer wide basin situated near the equator. It was a desolate, barren wasteland washed with a rose-colored hue. It had a terrible beauty. Ahead of them, somewhere to the west, lay the HAB, placed there by an earlier mission. It was their destination, their home for the next few months.

"We've got to move. Look." Paolio pointed over towards the horizon. Rolling across it was a vast billowing sandstorm. It was moving fast—in their direction. Commander Decker checked his holo-screen, a red blip pulsed out the HAB's location. He pointed off into the distance. "That way. Let's go."

They moved slowly, but with purpose. The last thing they needed was to be caught out in the open. Jann's sense of balance was fragile and she struggled to put one foot in front of the other. She felt like an ancient deep sea diver, trudging along an ocean floor hunting for pearls, weighed down with brass and lead.

"Malbec, pick up the pace, let's keep it moving," Decker's voice echoed in her head.

"Yes, commander."

Annis looked anxiously at the encroaching storm front. "We're not going to make it. Dammit. Looks like we figured it wrong. Anyway, we're committed now, no going back. Come on, we need to move faster."

Jann dug deep and found a rhythm of sorts. They moved

in silence, all focused on one objective, get to the HAB before the storm hit. She looked up at the ominous billowing cliff of dust as it moved and reshaped itself ever closer. Annis was right; they weren't going to make it.

"There it is." They could see the white squat cylinder of the HAB off in the distance, just before it was swallowed by the oncoming maelstrom.

"Stay close, we'll lose visibility shortly, everybody stay tight, keep everyone else in sight."

The storm charged across the crater's surface with impressive speed and Jann braced herself for impact. But the impact never came. The Martian atmosphere was so thin that she barely felt anything. It was eerie. Fine dust swirled everywhere and blocked out the world. Encapsulated in her EVA suit Jann had a strong feeling of dislocation. It was like she was not physically here. Like a ghost. She lost sight of all but Paolio and forced herself to move faster. Her balance failed, she tripped and tumbled forward.

"Help! I've fallen. I can't see anyone."

"Malbec, is that you? Goddammit, we don't need this now. Everyone stop exactly where you are. That includes you Malbec, don't move, we'll come to you, just stay put."

"I can't see anyone..." She managed to stand up again but had lost all sense of direction. Everywhere she looked was a dense murky sea of dust. She turned this way and that, arms outstretched. She was blind. Fear rose up inside her, she fought to control it. The sound of her own breathing began to reverberate in her helmet. She was beginning to panic.

A hand grabbed her elbow. "It's okay, Jann, I got you." It was Paolio. "Are you all right?"

Her breathing calmed. "I'm fine... just got a bit... I'm okay..." The others came into view, materializing out of the ghostly dust.

"Follow me, we're nearly there." Decker moved off again. The rest fell in behind. Jann stuck close to Paolio.

They walked for only a short time and finally the HAB rose up out of the dust like a lost ship in a fog. They found their way to the airlock door and one by one crossed the threshold and into safety. Decker hit the controls to pressurize the airlock. As soon as the alert flashed green the crew started to remove their helmets and breathe their first taste of HAB air.

"Holy crap," said Novack, "let's do that again."

2

JEZERO CRATER

For three days the vast Jezero Crater was immersed in dust as the crew waited it out, cocooned in the relative comfort of the HAB. It was a two story pressurized cylinder approximately eight meters in diameter and the same in height. The HAB was the culmination of intense design and redesign over thousands of hours and hundreds of iterations, each one inching it ever closer to ergonomic perfection. The ground floor housed the main operations area, a small galley dining space, and a utilitarian medlab sickbay. There was also a large airlock with enough room for all six crew along with EVA suits. An open column ran up the center of the HAB with a ladder and a small standing elevator, giving access to the top floor. It was divided into eight sections, sliced like a pie. It gave some private sleeping space for each crewmember along with a 'slice' each for exercise and sanitary. Compared to the cramped confines of the Odyssey it was palatial.

For Jann the sandstorm was a blessing in disguise as it gave her body time to adjust to working in one-third gravity. More than once she positioned an object in midair, expecting it to float, only for it to fall crashing to the floor. It also gave her mind time to contend with the enormity of the responsibility that lay before her. She spent much of this time in the privacy of her room studying mission protocol and mentally rehearsing many of the technical procedures.

By the morning of the fourth sol (day) the storm cleared, moving off eastward away from the crater basin. Jann sat in the HAB galley reading through the last known communication from Colony One. The message was sent over three and a half years ago by Nills Langthorp, the thirteenth human to set foot on Mars.

"What do you think he meant by that last line on the message?" Jann directed her question at Dr. Paolio Corelli, who was making his second espresso of the morning. The HAB had its own fresh coffee machine, courtesy of the Italian Space Agency. Paolio, being a native, was very proud of it and relished any opportunity to instruct the others as to its operation.

"Who... what line?"

"Nills Langthorp, the Mars colonist. His last message had the line Send no more."

Paolio waved his hand in the air. "Who knows? Many people have debated that over the last couple of years."

"I know, but what do you think it means?"

He sat down across from her and sipped his coffee with all the theater of a true connoisseur. "Most people think it meant send no more colonists. But I have another theory." He poked a finger in Jann's direction. "I think the message was cut off." He sat back.

"So you think there should be more to it?"

"Absolutely. I think what he was actually saying was send no more of that horrible Dutch coffee." He laughed.

Lu Chan stepped into the galley. "We'll be ready in ten for a preliminary mission brief."

"That gives me just enough time to show you how to use the espresso machine, Lu." Paolio jumped and grabbed a little cup from a storage unit.

"Paolio, show me later. I have to get ready for the brief."

"Nonsense, you have plenty of time."

Lu sighed. "Oh all right." She looked down at Jann. "Better let him show me so he doesn't keep going on about it." She rolled her eyes.

Lu and Paolio were close; they had a relaxed way with each other. Jann had considered it would be difficult for a relationship to survive the rigors of space travel. But they made it look easy. A part of her envied them. Paolio fussed and fiddled with the machine and a few minutes later Lu emerged from the huddle with a dainty little espresso.

"Come on guys, time for the brief." She brought her coffee with her.

THE SIX ISA crew gathered around a large display table in the operations area of the HAB and waited for Lu to start the session. She tapped an icon and a map of the Jezero Crater radiated out across the table surface. She tapped again and the map rendered itself in three dimensions. It gave the illusion of hovering above the surface of the table. She rotated it.

"This is us here." Lu pointed to a red marker overlaid on a 3D rendering of the HAB. She zoomed in. "Over here is the lander and that's our fuel processing plant."

"Okay, let's see Colony One," said Commander Decker. The map zoomed out and they could now see most of the western side of the crater.

"That's Colony One, about two kilometers west, near the crater's edge." She rotated the map and zoomed in on the site. A wire frame 3D model ballooned out from the display table. "I can overlay this with our latest orbiter imagery to give us a better idea of what we can expect."

The Colony One site slowly rendered itself in photo-quality detail. It was a sizable facility comprised of a large biodome where the colonists had grown most of the food that sustained them. Radiating around this was a number of smaller domes and around these were dotted a series of interconnected modules, arranged like petals on a flower. These were the landers that each batch of six colonists arrived in.

"As you can see, the roof of this dome here has caved in, and the same with this one. We have major sand ingress here and here. Also several of these modules are damaged or missing completely." They looked at the model as it rotated slowly. It was more detailed than anything they had seen before.

"How can modules just disappear, could they have blown away?" said Jann.

"Impossible, the atmosphere is too thin for even the most vicious sandstorm to do that. The only explanation is they moved them or maybe they dismantled them for some other purpose," said Lu.

"These long humps in the sand are more grow areas, right?"

"One is. The other is soil processing for water reclamation and resource extraction—and it looks like that has also collapsed." Lu zoomed out from the main structure to take in more of the surrounding area.

"Over here, on the edge of the site is the main solar array field—looks about eighty percent intact. Here, up on the crater's edge is the plutonium reactor. We need to be very careful of this, in case it's fractured. The power cables run down along here and across here.

"I presume that's the last supply ship?" said Decker.

"Yes, still exactly where it landed, untouched for over three years."

In the months after contact was lost with Colony One, an unmanned ship was sent packed with emergency supplies, in the vain hope that some of the colonists might be still alive. It was still there where it landed, gathering dust —literally.

"I count six bodies, but none near the reactor or along the cable routes."

"I wonder why they're all scattered around like that?" Paolio waved a hand around the 3D map.

"If they went out during the sandstorm there would have been very poor visibility. They probably got disorientated. A bit like Malbec did when we arrived here," said the commander with a laugh. Jann said nothing.

"Lu can you zoom in a bit more on this body here?" said Paolio. The map model ballooned out and picked up on the prostrate form of a dead colonist. It lay flat on its back.

"I could be mistaken, but he, or she, looks to be missing an arm."

"Well the image at this detail is poor so it could just be a buildup of sand around the body obscuring the arm." Lu leaned to examine the image.

"I don't think so," said Paolio.

"Why?"

"Because... I think that's it over there." He pointed to an arm shaped smudge a few meters from the body.

The others looked at the forlorn figure with a mixture of fascination and horror.

"Well, we'll find out for sure soon enough." Commander Decker reached over and shut off the map. "Okay, listen up. I want all system checks done on all the equipment as soon as possible. Once everything is nominal we can proceed to the site. You all know what to do, this is what we trained for so lets get to it." He clapped his hands together.

"And Malbec…"

"Yes, commander?"

"I need you to stay sharp. I know you haven't had a lot of training but I still want you focused."

"Yes. Of course, commander."

"Why does he give me such a hard time?" Jann and Lu were in full EVA suits, outside on the planet's surface, running diagnostic tests on the two utility rovers.

"He just wants to keep on top of the mission. Take my advice, don't take it personally." Lu disengaged the rover locking mechanisms to wake them up.

"Maybe you're right."

"I *am* right. You try too hard, Jann. No one's expecting you to be perfect at everything. Just keep your head down, stay focused and you'll be fine."

"I wish I had your confidence."

Lu stopped and looked over at her. "Believe me, underneath this elegant, swan-like exterior there's a lot of paddling going on." She laughed.

"Okay, I get it, head down, stay focused."

"Exactly... and chill out."

"And chill out." She nodded and smiled at Lu.

"That's the important bit."

That said, Jann was finding it difficult to concentrate on the task at hand. In fact, both of them would get distracted, and stop and look around at the Martian landscape. It was the first time that Jann really had a chance to truly look at her surroundings. The trip from the lander to the HAB had been one of sheer terror, not a time for sightseeing.

"It's incredible, isn't it?" she said.

"Yes, truly awe inspiring." Lu was staring off into the distance. The topography of the crater basin was mainly flat with dips and valleys undulating across it. They could see Isidis Peak off to the east. To the west, the rim of the crater looped around the horizon. They stood there for quite some time, soaking in the vista.

After a while they turned back to their work. Lu hit a button on her remote control display and the first rover rolled out from its compartment onto the dusty soil. These were heavy-duty utility vehicles used for transporting equipment, supplies and samples. They were not designed for driving around in by crew. Just simple robotic mules, the space exploration equivalent of flatbed carts. Jann poked a button on her remote and the second rover rolled out. She drove it out a few meters from the base of the HAB and set to work doing a full systems test. Both rovers had robotic arms but one mule also had a drill for seismic research. The colonists had discovered cave systems in the area, so this rover was here to find and map these. It could drill down to a depth of several meters and deposit an explosive charge. When it detonated, the resultant shock wave would be analyzed and a detailed chart rendered of the subsurface.

They were also designed to be autonomous. You could load one up with all your gear, set a beacon on your EVA suit and the rover should follow along wherever you went—like a faithful donkey. Jann was now testing this; she walked away from the HAB and the rover dutifully followed. However, the terrain around the HAB was hard and flat, easy ground for the rover. What she needed was something more rugged to truly put the machine through its paces. Jann looked out across the vast crater basin and marched off in search of more testing ground.

After the months of confinement onboard the Odyssey, on top of months of intensive training before that, she now felt a wave of exhilarating freedom wash over her. The vast plain stretched out as far as the eye could see: desolate, empty and inviting. She felt like a child again, wandering off across an expanse of old family farm. She moved with a steady, easy pace, soaking up her surroundings as she went, lost in her thoughts.

"Jann, where are you off to?" Lu's voice broke into her reverie.

"Oh... eh." She had to think for a moment to orientate herself. "I'm just testing the rover... taking it for a walk."

"You don't have to take it to the other side of the planet. Try and remember the focus part, Jann."

"Okay... yes. I'll head back." She took one last look out across the crater before turning around.

"Focus, I really need to keep focused."

3

COLONY ONE

It took most of that morning to get all the system checks complete. Once finished, Decker reported back to mission control, and by late morning they received a go to proceed with a preliminary reconnaissance of the derelict Colony One site. An air of excitement rippled through the crew as they suited up in the airlock.

"Comms check." Decker's voice squawked in Jann's helmet, followed by a ripple of verbal affirmations by the rest of the crew.

"Listen up. I want a tight line, no wandering off and no falling behind, Malbec. Understood?"

Jann nodded and they exited the airlock, stepping out onto the Martian surface. They wasted no time in loading up one of the rovers with the necessary equipment and, with final checks done, Decker gave the command to move out.

The six crew of the ISA Mars mission marched off in the direction of the crater rim, the location of Colony One.

Reconnaissance imagery depicted the crater basin to be smooth and flat, but on the ground it varied widely. The terrain ahead undulated with dips and valleys, while underfoot it shifted from hard cracked regolith to soft sandy dunes. Rocks and boulders of varying size and composition were scattered across the entire site. Walking in one-third gravity took some getting used to and Jann, as usual, had difficulty keeping pace. It didn't help that she would get distracted by the landscape and slow down to take it all in. More than once Decker halted the procession just so she could catch up.

"Hey... check this out." Chief Engineer, Kevin Novack, looked down at the ground and toed some object in the dirt.

"What have you found?" said Annis.

"If I'm not mistaken, it looks like litter." He reached down, tugged the edge of a plastic bag buried in the soil and pulled it out. "A component wrapper of some kind." The others gathered around. They could just make out the faded Colony One Mars (COM) logo on the outside. Decker paid no attention to the artifact, he was busy scanning the horizon.

"There it is... over there," he pointed in the direction of a rock formation nestled in front of a low line of dunes. Through a dip in the line they could just make out the top of the biodome.

"Let's keep moving." He started off again.

Novack wasn't sure what to do with the wrapper. In the end he just let it fall out of his gloved hand and it drifted back down onto the sand. They moved off towards their destination.

After a while, it became apparent to them that the rock formation in the foreground was not natural. It seemed to have been constructed by someone, a colonist presumably. Annis was first there to investigate. "It looks like a small hut, crudely built with rocks, like an old stone wall." Annis paused, gently ran her hand over the stones and then continued with her commentary. "It's around two meters high and the same wide... with a domed roof. There's an opening on this side. I'm going in."

"Wait, Annis! It may be unstable, you shouldn't take any unnecessary risks just yet." Jann's voice squawked in the first officer's comm. Annis hesitated for a moment, looked over at Jann and then back at the hut. It was like she was considering a reply, but thought better of it and entered the stone hut regardless.

"There's a body in here... just sitting in the middle of the floor," she announced.

Jann was next over to peer inside, although she stood some way back, just in case her futile warning to Annis turned out to be prophetic.

A colonist in a full EVA suit sat cross-legged in the center of the small space, its head slumped down a little on to its chest. The nametag on the left breast read Bess Keilly. They all gathered around the strange alien mausoleum for a time, in silence, taking turns to peer in at the dead occupant.

"It's a beehive hut," said Kevin after a while. This seemed to snap them all out of it.

"What is?" said Annis.

"The little building here." He waved a hand over the hut.

"You mean for bees?" said Lu.

"No, not for bees—for monks," said Kevin. "There's a tiny remote island off the westernmost tip of Ireland—Skellig Michael it's called. A group of monks set up housekeeping on it back in the 6th century. They lived in huts built just like this one. They're called beehive huts because of the shape." He waved an arm around again. "The island was regarded as the most remote place in the known world."

"I don't get it, why would anyone build such a thing here?" said Lu.

"It's a sculpture, I suppose. A piece of art. It obviously has no useful purpose," offered Kevin.

"Well they did have a lot of time on their hands. Seems completely pointless to me," said Decker. "Okay, let's keep going."

They left the grim Celtic crypt and climbed up the back of a high dune. The sand was loose and their boots sank in as they progressed up its side. It made for tough going. Jann was last to crest the dune. She stopped at the peak and looked in awe as the entire Colony One site sprawled out before her.

"Wow, it looks way bigger than I imagined," she said. Jann could now see where some of the domes had caved in. Sand had also built up around the derelict site and it looked like Mars was reclaiming it, inch by inch, a little bit more with each passing year. It was like discovering the remains of some long lost alien civilization on a far off planet. And, in many respects, that's exactly what it was.

One by one, they descended the side of the low dune into the basin of the site and fanned out across its expanse. Jann felt like she was entering an abandoned mining town. Equipment strewn here and there, along with odd rock formations and sculptures of one kind or another. Most were in a state of collapse and partly covered in sand. On the far edge of the site, out past the solar array field, Jann could see the last supply lander, still sitting where it came down, untouched.

For a time they wandered aimlessly around the site in a kind of dazed wonder. Like how Howard Carter must have felt after entering the tomb of Tutankhamen.

"Found another body." Dr. Corelli's voice reverberated in Jann's helmet. He was bending over the prostrate corpse of a dead colonist. It was lying face up, visor smashed, and was missing an arm just below the shoulder.

"It looks like a clean cut..." Paolio was examining the injury. "...done with something very sharp."

By now some of the other crew had gathered around. "Seems you were right, Doctor," said the commander. "The arm is over there." He pointed at the dismembered limb a few feet away.

"What the hell happened here?" said Annis.

"Well it wasn't the sandstorm, that for sure," said Jann.

"Obviously," replied Decker. "Okay, we need to stick with the program. I want everybody on heads-up. The commander thumbed a button on his suit sleeve. The others did the same. On her visor Jann could now see an illuminated three dimensional wire-frame overlay of the site. It followed the contours of the buildings as she moved, giving detailed information on each structure. There were also five flashing markers tracking each of the other crewmembers.

"Paolio, Lu, Jann, take a route around the northern perimeter of the structure. Myself, Annis and Kevin will explore the area on this side. We'll meet up over at the main airlock." He pointed off at a group of modules attached to the main Colony One dome. "Let's get to it."

"What about the mule?" said Jann.

"Just keep it tagged to you, we may need it on the other side."

"You're not planning on going inside the facility today, are you?" said Annis.

Decker considered this. "We'll see... after we do an inspection. It's a derelict site so it may be too dangerous. Anyway, let's get a move on."

They split up. Paolio took the lead and they walked over towards what remained of humanity's first ever planetary outpost. The structure was dominated by a massive bio-dome. Around this were the smaller domes, and around these were attached the crew landers and supply modules that the colonists and equipment arrived in. These were cylindrical, around five or so meters wide and the same tall. They each had two doors and some also had airlocks. They could be attached together and reconfigured into different arrangements. Somewhere on the far side of the structure were two long grow tunnels, partially buried in the sand. One of these had collapsed.

The first lander module they came to Jann's heads-up display identified as simply EVA/Maintenance, an entrance in and out of the base for work crews. A sand ramp had been built up to the height of the airlock entrance and the outer door was wide open. She walked up the ramp and peered inside. The inner door into the facility was sealed tight. The interior, having been exposed to the Martian weather, was covered in a thick buildup of sand and dust.

"Come and have a look at this." She waved her arm to signal Paolio and Lu. Inside the airlock, bolted to the floor, was a rudimentary windmill, fashioned from recycled materials. Its crude blades sat motionless in the still atmosphere.

"Weird. What do you think that was for?" said Paolio.

"Generating power, I think. Look there's a wire leading in through the door seal," Jann traced the cable with her gloved hand.

"But there's no wind."

"Not today, but during a sandstorm there would be plenty of wind. See the size of the vanes, big to catch as much as possible. They must have been desperate to generate more power," said Jann.

"Looks like it, although they wouldn't get very much from this. To generate any sort of meaningful power on Mars it would need to be massive." Lu was examining the motionless blades.

They moved away from the airlock and continued their circumnavigation of the facility perimeter. "Over here," said Paolio as he waved to the others. "It's an old rover."

A small, six wheeled machine was partly buried in sand. Two circular solar panels extended from its back, giving it the look of a winged insect. It was covered in grime. Jann wiped a hand over a panel to brush the dust off. She thought she saw a green LED flash momentarily and jumped back in fright. "Holy shit. I think it's still working."

"You okay?" said Paolio.

"Fine... just a bit jittery."

Lu laughed. "That rover hasn't functioned in years. It's totally dead, for sure."

As they moved away, Jann looked back at the little machine, half expecting it to awaken and crawl out of its sandy grave.

The three were now close to the base of the main biodome. It had a wall about two meters high made of a type of concrete produced in-situ from the local regolith. It was robotically manufactured and had been layered down by large industrial sized 3D printers. The upper dome structure consisted of a super-tough, semi-transparent membrane stretched over a lattice framework, its complex molecular structure engineered to provide radiation shielding. It was essentially the same material used in one of the many layers of the crews' EVA suits.

Jann walked up the edge of the wall where the sand had built up, in the hope that she could see in. But so much grime had accumulated on the surface that it was impossible to make anything out.

They moved on towards one of the smaller domes where the roof had collapsed. The support members were bent and crumpled. Jann's augmented reality display overlaid a wire-frame of the last known facility configuration. On the readout there should have been three modules attached, tagged accommodation. But they were missing.

"See, the wall here has been sealed up. So they must have moved the modules," said Paolio.

"I wonder where are they?" said Jann.

"Recycled maybe, broken up and used inside for something."

As they worked their way around they could see several more modules were missing. On the far side of the facility, leading from the base of the biodome, the two long grow tunnels extended outward. These were partially covered in

Martian soil. This was one of the oldest parts of the colony, built even before the first colonists arrived. They had been robotically constructed prior to human habitation so that the early settlers would have sufficient infrastructure to maximize their chances of survival.

Jann had considered simply walking over one in the hope that she would be high enough to get a glimpse through the main dome membrane, but thought better of it. The tunnel was probably fragile and one of them had already collapsed. Also the weight of the mule following along behind her might be too much for it. She instead walked around the tunnels. It was difficult to know where they ended as they seemed to just merge into the surrounding dunes. The crew gave them a wide berth nonetheless.

By the time they headed back to the main dome they could see Decker and the others approaching the cluster of four modules grouped together. A sand ramp led up to the main airlock. But unlike the others they had inspected, the door was shut tight.

"Malbec, bring that mule over here," said Decker. "Tell me we brought the laser cutters, Kevin."

"We did, why, what are you planning?" replied the engineering officer.

"A little breaking and entering."

Jann untagged the mule so it would stay put and not follow her around anymore. Kevin started to unload equipment cases.

"I don't think that will be necessary." Annis pulled the recessed handle on the airlock door and it swung open. She stepped through and examined the inner panel.

"That's odd."

"What is?" The commander was now beside her in the airlock.

"It's got power."

"Well that's possible, since the solar array field looks mostly undamaged."

"It's not just that... it looks like... well, it's pressurized inside."

"Let me see." The chief engineer was now examining the panel. He rubbed a layer of dust off the small screen and stood back in amazement. "I think you're right."

"All right," said Decker, "here's what we're going to do. Kevin, bring that cutting gear in here. We'll need to close the outer door before we can open the inner one. If we can't get it open, we'll cut it open. If we get stuck in here, we'll cut our way out. The rest of you wait outside until I give the all clear." He stopped for a moment, then looked at each of them in turn. "You all need to prepare yourselves for what we'll find in here. There's probably going to be a lot of dead bodies. It isn't going to be pretty so be ready."

They all nodded. Jann had not given this much thought. But now that the time had come, it was clear that it would be a hellish tableau that greeted them on the inside. She imagined the desperate colonists huddled together in some corner of the facility, eking out the last of their precious resources, all hope lost, waiting for death to come.

Decker, Annis and Kevin stepped inside the airlock and closed the outer door. Jann and the others could hear the conversation through their helmet comms. She looked over at Lu and Paolio. They exchanged a glance that spoke of excited apprehension.

"Outer door sealed, okay... let's see if this works." It was Kevin's voice. "Look, it's pressurizing, there must really be air in there, incredible. Sixty percent... eighty... hundred. All right, here goes... opening inner door." There was a pause in the chief engineer's commentary as he surveyed the interior. Jann, Lu and Paolio waited anxiously for him to resume.

"Looks like a storage area... boxes piled up on either side. Some old EVA suits... torn... parts missing... no helmets that I can see. Moving into the next section. Seems to be a common area... seating... tables. Wait a minute... that's impossible!"

"What, what is?" said Lu.

"Eh... you guys better get in here and see this for yourselves," said Decker.

4

EXPLORATION

Jann opened the exterior airlock door and stepped in, followed closely by Lu and Paolio, who shut the outer door behind him and spun the locking wheel. Jann hit the button to equalize pressure. It took a few anxious moments to complete the cycle and for the green alert light to illuminate. "Okay, here goes," she said, as she swung open the inner door. They passed through the airlock and Jann, Lu and Paolio stepped into Colony One.

They passed through the entrance into a room lined with broken and damaged EVA suits. They hung along the walls like abandoned marionettes. Ahead of them the area opened out and pale orange sunlight filtered down through the domed roof, illuminating a large circular space. It looked like a junkyard. Every available flat surface was covered with machines and components in varying states of disassembly.

Balls of wire sprouted from containers and spooled out across the floor. Tubes and pipes snaked around the area in all directions. Yet, it was clear that a routine had been well worn into this apparent chaos.

They spotted the others just ahead.

"Over here," Kevin beckoned to them and pointed at something on one of the benches. "Have a look at this."

They gathered around and inspected the object that had so startled the commander. Resting on a plate, beside a small box of fresh fruit, an apple had been cut in two, a bite taken from one half. Kevin held the knife up and they could see the juice ruining down along the edge. "It's just been cut."

There was a stunned silence for a moment as the implications began to sink in. Jann reached down, picked up the partially eaten apple and held it up close to her visor so she could give it a better examination. It was fresh, no doubt about it.

"There's someone here, still alive. That's incredible," said Jann. "How is that possible, after all this time?" She put the apple back down on the bench.

By now, they were all looking around, expecting the ragged survivors to come through a door or emerge from some darkened alcove at any moment. Jann considered that the joy of the crew's arrival could be overwhelming for them. Like a group of deserted island castaways rescued after many years of isolation. So they waited with ever mounting anticipation—but no one showed.

"Where the hell are they?" said Annis.

"Maybe they're afraid?" ventured Kevin.

"Of what?"

No one had an answer.

"Okay, there's someone still alive here, that much is certain. So, if they won't come to us then we'll just have to go to them. We need to do a full search of this facility, every inch of it if necessary, starting with the biodome over there." Decker pointed towards an open tunnel at the far end of the space. "Let's go." He marched off.

They picked their way through the junkyard detritus towards the entrance and passed into the low connecting tunnel. One by one, they entered into the biodome into a sea of verdant vegetation. Row upon row of food crops radiated out across the vast space. Densely packed grow-beds were built into racks stacked one on top of the other—three, sometimes four layers high. Tubes coiled around each bed bringing water and nutrients to the plants. A confusion of power lines and ducting arched overhead. Grow lights hung from beneath each row to augment the pale Martian sunlight. It was a machine for growing food. Everywhere was ordered and meticulously maintained, in complete contrast to the mayhem of the previous area.

"Wow, just look at this place, it's incredible," said Lu as the six ISA crew stood around in awe at the lush surroundings.

"We should split up," said the commander. "Paolio, Jann,

take that side, and check out that long grow tunnel. But be careful, though. It may be structurally compromised. Kevin, Lu, you search along the opposite side, over there. Annis and I will take this central area. Let's see if we can find some life forms in here other than plants."

A PATH WOUND its way around the inside perimeter of the dome; Jann and Paolio followed it. Along the inner wall were stacked storage boxes of one kind or another. Jann opened one, it was full of some sort of biomass, and she wasn't sure what it was without testing.

"Potatoes," Paolio pointed at long neat rows of plants. "And carrots." They walked through the rows for a while, identifying some as they went. "I recognize this," said Paolio. Jann looked at the leafy plant. "Is that what I think it is?" she said as she touched a leaf.

"Cannabis. Presumably it's legal on Mars," said Paolio.

Jann laughed. "I suppose the law is what you decide yourself up here. Looks like someone brought some seeds with them. They're healthy plants, so whoever is here is looking after them."

Paolio looked around. "So we're looking for a bunch of Martian stoners—wherever the hell they are."

"Come on, let's keep looking."

After a while it became evident to Jann that there were a great many plants she simply did not recognize. These, she suspected, were genetically engineered specifically for Colony One. Designed to produce food in the weak Martian sun. Plants that would never be allowed free reign on Earth, due to concerns over genetic contamination. But here, there were no such fears. As a biologist, she had followed the development of some of these new botanical species with avid interest. Colony One was a geneticist's playground, with a totally controlled eco-system, and not bound by the ethics of Earth. There really was no law on Mars but your own.

THEY ARRIVED at a point along the dome wall where it opened into one of the long buried tunnels. It had a wide airlock, but both doors were swung fully open.

Jann took a cautious step inside. It was wide, with dim overhead lighting. Two long rows of clear plastic water tanks receded into its depths. They could see that each one contained a different species of fish. The tanks all looked to be well stocked. The fish looked to be perfectly healthy. Towards the back of the tunnel she found several low, shallow beds used for spawning.

"This is very impressive. It takes a lot of skill and knowledge to be able to do this," said Jann.

"I wonder if they're genetically engineered?" Paolio was leaning over a tank looking down at the swimming fish.

"That's a possibility. Although I didn't hear of it. Still, they were very secretive about what they were doing up here."

．　．　．

"IF YOU'RE FINISHED your sweep, meet us in the middle. There's something here you should see." Decker's voice echoed in Jann's helmet. She nodded over at Paolio and they both made for the rendezvous point in the middle of the dome.

"It's getting very hot in this suit." Jann was looking at the temperature readout on her helmet's biometric display. The EVA suit was designed to keep the occupant warm on the surface of Mars, where it could often be minus sixty. But in the hot and humid environment of the biodome the suit was having trouble maintaining a comfortable level. "We're going to have to get out of here soon."

"Yeah, I'm boiling up."

As they moved closer to the middle of the vast space, the neat rows of hydroponics gave way to an overgrown wilderness. The plants in this section had been let to run rampant. Yet here and there could be seen a deliberate planting structure. Someone designed it this way. Tall trees and grasses lined the path and, as they neared the center, branches began to hang down and form a tunnel. It was covered with trailing vines.

"It's like a tropical glasshouse in some botanic garden," said Jann, as she brushed her gloved hand along the hanging tendrils.

The path ended and they stepped out onto a large central

dais. It was wide and flat. At the far end it sloped into a sizable pond, with a three meter high waterfall that sparkled and danced in the pale sunlight. The others were gathered around a hammock slung between two trees. Below it, on a low table, was a control interface of some kind. Kevin was down on one knee investigating.

"This is amazing," said Jann looking around.

"It's like Paradise Island," replied Paolio.

"Decker looked over at them. "Anything?"

"No, nothing. Just fish."

"Maybe they really *are* hiding from us," ventured Lu.

"Someone's here—somewhere." Decker was looking at a schematic of the facility on a small tablet screen.

"I'm burning up in this suit, we can't stay here much longer." Annis was also getting uncomfortable.

"Dammit, I don't want to report to mission control that the place is functioning and colonists are still alive but we can't find them," said Decker.

"We may have to. We need to get out of here and back to the HAB. We can do a better search tomorrow." Annis was moving off towards the airlock.

"Wait a minute." With that, Decker reached for the side of his helmet to flip open the visor.

"No... wait... don't do that. The air could be poisonous in here. We need to do some analysis first."

"It's fine, Paolio. Someone's alive in here so they must be breathing good air, right?

"You don't know that for sure."

Decker ignored him and popped his visor open. He held his breath for a second or two and then took his first gulp of Colony One air. The others waited. He smiled, laughed and breathed again. Then he sniffed. "It smells like... like a forest."

Annis was next to pop her visor. She took a deep breath and then removed her helmet completely, shaking out her long hair. "Oh my god, that's better. I was beginning to feel like a hot dog in a water bath."

Kevin was next and soon they all had their helmets off. Jann was last to open her visor and breathe the fragrant air. Decker was right. It smelled of botanicals and biomass. It was strange that a colony outpost, on a far off planet, should have such a smell. It reminded Jann of an exotic garden.

Decker removed his gloves. "Okay, this gives us a lot more time to do a thorough search of the facility and find these people." He was back to consulting his screen.

"I don't think they want to be found," said Jann.

"That doesn't make any sense. Why not? They've just endured three and a half years isolated here with no communication," said Annis.

"Maybe they've gone insane—you know, and think we're a bunch of aliens invading the planet," offered Kevin.

Decker ignored these comments. "We still haven't searched any of the modules along these other sections. I suggest two of us stay here and keep an eye on the door into the dome. The rest of us will continue the search."

I'll stay here, if that's okay," said Lu.

"Fine, Kevin can keep you company. The rest of you... let's go, let's find these people."

There were a myriad of other modules connected to smaller domes, all grouped in different configurations. The first group they came to seemed to be used for refrigerated storage of some kind. Jann opened one of the large doors. "There's no point in that, Jann. We're not looking for a snowman." Decker laughed at his own joke. Then he stopped, gripped his abdomen and bent over with a low groan.

"Commander, what is it?" said Paolio.

He stood upright again. "It's nothing, just a bit dehydrated I think."

"Let me have a look at you."

Decker brushed him away. "I'm fine, it's nothing." With that he doubled over again clutching his stomach."

"You're not fine, let me see you." Paolio examined the commander as best he could. He felt his pulse and then put the back of his hand on Decker's forehead. "You're burning up. We need to get you back to the HAB—right now."

This time the commander didn't protest. He was leaning against the module wall, slowly sliding down onto the floor.

"Jann, give me a hand here." Paolio was throwing

Decker's arm around his shoulder. Jann grabbed the other side and they helped him up.

"We need to go," said Paolio, as he and Jann helped Decker walk back to the entrance airlock.

"Lu, Kevin, you both better get out here," said Annis. There was no mistaking the note of urgency in her voice.

"What's happened?" said Lu when she saw them holding Decker up.

"The commander is not feeling well. Everyone put their helmets on—now. We're heading back to the HAB."

They carried Decker into the airlock. He was conscious but seemed to be having intermittent cramps and would double over in pain when they struck.

Once the crew were all back outside on the surface Annis hit a button on her remote. The rover awoke and started across the site towards them. They bundled the commander into the back of the rover and started off. "We'd better hurry," said Paolio. The rover bumped and rocked over the Martian terrain as they all pushed hard for the HAB. Decker was bounced around and lapsed in and out of consciousness. Jann watched all this from her permanent place as last in line. No one spoke.

ONCE INSIDE THE HAB they got the commander out of his EVA suit and laid him on a bed in the tiny medical bay. He was now unconscious. Paolio shooed the others away and started his examination. The crew retreated into the operations area.

"Anyone else feel unwell?" Annis had assumed command now that Decker was non-operational, as she put it. Grunts and head shakes rippled around the crew as they eyed each other like a clandestine group seeking out a spy in their midst. They were all okay—for now. The crew sat in silence for a long time, waiting for the verdict from Paolio.

"So what the hell is it?" Annis was pacing; it was a habit of hers. The doctor had finished his examination and re-entered the operations area.

"I think it's possibly an allergic reaction. But he's stable now and I reckon he'll be okay, once it passes."

An audible sigh of relief emanated from the assembled crew.

"Do you think it was the air in the Colony?" Annis continued.

"I don't think so, since everyone else seems fine. But, it's not possible to know for sure without some further analysis. Now, if you don't mind, I need a stiff coffee." He moved off to fire up the espresso machine.

"Everyone else is okay, aren't they?" Annis looked around at the rest of the crew. They all nodded. Yet Jann knew they were all thinking the same thing. "Only time will tell."

5

VANHOFF

Peter VanHoff, president of the Colony One Mars consortium, stood watching the snow fall from a window high up in his isolated Norwegian mansion. It swirled and danced under the garden lights, accumulating where it lay, like a soft duvet blanketing the earth. He turned away from the window and set about poking the log fire that was burning in the hearth. Sparks flared up with each thrust of the fire iron. He hung it back on its stand and sat himself in a high-backed leather armchair. Winter had thrust its first icy fingers into the landscape. He liked this time. The natural world slowed down, hibernated. He felt it resonated with his condition and held it in check.

Born with a rare genetic disorder akin to progeria, he aged at an accelerated rate. He was only thirty-eight, yet he looked fifty plus. Peter touched the back of his hand, the parchment skin, the genetically flawed epidermis—an ever-present reminder of his affliction. Was it improving? Was it getting worse? He couldn't tell. At least maintaining the status quo was better than succumbing to the inevitable entropy of his condition.

Yet what would have been a curse for some, Peter VanHoff turned into a crusade, dedicating himself to the genetic understanding of the aging process, becoming one of the foremost experts in the process. His research corporation made numerous early breakthroughs, resulting in lucrative patents and a considerable fortune for VanHoff. However, his greatest strides were made through the association with the Colony One Mars consortium, COM for short. This commercial partnership enabled his corporation to conduct research on Mars that simply wasn't ethical on earth.

His ruminations were interrupted by the chime of his holo-tab. The screen flickered with a muted illumination and an icon rotated above its surface. He had a call—Nagle Bagleir, vice president of COM. What could he want at this time of night? Several disaster scenarios ran through VanHoff's mind as he waved a hand across the screen. Nagle's avatar shimmered into existence in the air over the tablet's surface, and spoke.

"Extraordinary news, Peter. It looks as if Colony One is not as dead as we thought."

Peter sat bolt upright and fumbled with his glasses. There was a moment's silence as he considered this revelation. "What... alive... are you saying there are colonists still alive up there?"

"Not quite. But we've just got a report in from the ISA crew. A significant portion of the facility is still intact and functioning. It also looks like there are signs of survivors, but we have no confirmation on that just yet."

"After all this time—but this is impossible." The implications of the discovery began to filter through Peter VanHoff's stunned brain. "What about the research lab? Is that still intact?"

"We don't know anything about the lab just yet. What we do know is it's going to be all over the news in less than an hour. The ISA have scheduled a press conference for 1:30am, your time."

"This is incredible." VanHoff stood up and began to pace. "If that lab is intact then there's a possibility that the research data still exists."

"My thoughts exactly."

Peter's voice became hushed. "We can't let that fall into the wrong hands."

"As in the ISA?"

"You know who I mean. Everything the ISA does is in the public domain. Anything they find up there can't be kept hidden."

"Well, it's a bit late for that now. You know as well as I do that after the collapse of the colony we had no option but to hand it all over to them. Otherwise we wouldn't be back up there now." Nagle's avatar shimmered as it spoke. "That said, we do have some contingencies on-site, Peter. But yes, I agree, we wouldn't want it becoming public."

"This is extraordinary. If that data still exists..." VanHoff didn't finish the sentence.

"There's another thing. It may be nothing, then again..."

"What?"

"One of the crew has become ill."

"Not our agent, I trust?"

"No, the ISA Commander, Decker."

"Is it the same symptoms as... you know?"

"Let's not jump to conclusions just yet. Like I said, it could be nothing."

There was a pause as VanHoff considered all this information. Nagle continued. "In light of these developments, I suggest reconvening the board."

"Agreed, absolutely."

"You are of course aware that there will be certain members getting jittery with this news, Peter. You know who I'm talking about."

VanHoff grunted. "That research may be more significant to humanity than the discovery of alien life."

"Be that as it may. But we've been all working under the premise that it was dead and buried—forever. This changes everything."

VanHoff stopped pacing the floor. "You're right, Nagle, let's not be too hasty. Let's see how things develop. After all, we have our agent on site. That may prove to be a very wise decision after all."

"Yes, it may. I must sign off now; I need to alert the others. I'll keep you posted on the meeting." The avatar that was Nagle extinguished itself like a church candle in a draft.

BEFORE PETER VANHOFF took over control of COM, the original members were an eclectic mix of Mars enthusiasts, scientists and captains of industry that shared a common dream—to establish a human colony on Mars and lay the foundations for mankind as an interplanetary species. It had helped that most of them were newly minted tech billionaires. Yet, this in itself was not enough to launch a mission to the red planet. The complexities, and cost, of sending and returning humans had been such that no national space agency, at that time, could entertain it with any real vigor. NASA tried but its timelines kept being pushed out further and further. As one commentator put it, "We're ten years away from landing on Mars. And regardless of what decade you ask me this, we'll still be ten years away."

But COM had the advantage of being a private company, not bound by the politics of electoral consensus or the restraints of governmental budgets. They were also increasingly frustrated by the lack of progress in manned space exploration since the first moon landings. And so they conceived of a radical plan to establish a human colony on the red planet. Its success pivoted on one simple operational premise—remove the need to return. They would send humans to Mars, but they would not come back. The colonists would live out the rest of their natural lives looking up at Earth from 140 million miles away.

Of those early colonists, some said they were naive. Others said they were the embodiment of the human spirit. But many simply regarded them as crazy. Who in their right mind would go to Mars in the full knowledge that they could never return? Yet, potential colonists applied in their thousands and the stage was set for the greatest human adventure of all time.

In the early days, COM sought to fund these missions by turning the colonization of Mars into a reality TV show. They broadcast and streamed everything from the selection process and training, to the first liftoff and daily life on the red planet. It was a slow start but it proved to be an inspired move. As far as the viewers were concerned, it was people power writ large in the heavens, and boy did they love it. As ever more colonists made their way to Mars, their every word, every thought, every mundane activity was recorded, digitized, broadcast and analyzed by the masses back on earth. Everyone who watched these incredible events had an opinion, and not all of them were favorable. Yet, in the end, even the most strident critics of the Colony One Mars adventure eventually succumbed to reluctant admiration. There was no denying it was the dawn of a new era for humanity, an era where the zeitgeist reveled in the optimism for the future of the human race. Just think, if we the people could do this then there was nothing that we couldn't do.

For a long time this mood prevailed as Colony One grew and prospered. Until the mother of all sandstorms hit. It darkened the sky and blasted the colony for a full six months. Communication became sporadic in frequency and erratic in content. There were rumors of colonists suffering mental breakdown, going crazy even. Concern was building back on Earth, and as the weeks and months passed, this concern grew into fear. Fear that Colony One, and those who called it home, were being etched off the surface of the planet, one grain of sand at a time, like an hourglass running down.

Attempts at satellite imagery during this period were futile. So it was a full six months after the storm when the first high-resolution images of the site were released to the public. They showed devastation. Worse, bodies of several colonists could be seen lying around the facility. It was clear that Colony One had totally collapsed as a human outpost. That was three and a half years ago.

An hour after Peter VanHoff finished his call with Nagle Bagleir, the news of the discovery broke on an unsuspecting world. It was a media frenzy.

6

HAB

Jann couldn't sleep. She tossed and turned, and thumped her pillow a few times to try and beat some comfort into it. It didn't work. She lay on her back and stared at the roof of the HAB for a while, but there wasn't much to look at. The sleeping compartment was cramped, like all the others. Some would find it even a little claustrophobic, but that wasn't something she suffered from. Being an astronaut was not a job option for anyone who had a fear of enclosed spaces. She sat up. There was no point in forcing it. If she couldn't sleep she might as well get up and raid the galley for some comfort food, not that there was any. Unless you counted coffee, but it was a bit late for that. She still had hopes of a few hours sleep before taking on the trials of tomorrow.

She clambered out of bed and made her way to the

access column, descending the ladder to the main deck below. In the dim light she could see Paolio sitting at the low galley table. He looked like he was reading.

"Jann, can't sleep?"

"No, I've given up, for the moment."

"Like an espresso?"

"God no. I'd be even more wired."

"This is a myth, I can drink coffee any time and still fall asleep."

"That's because you're Italian—anyway, you're still awake."

"Ha, yes... it's because I've not had enough coffee yet to put me to sleep." He laughed lightly.

Jann smiled. She nodded in the direction of the slumbering commander. "How is he?"

"Good, I'm just keeping an eye on him. But I think he'll be fine. His vitals have stabilized."

Jann took a juice and a small oat bar from a storage compartment and sat down across from the doctor. She sighed.

"So how are you doing, Jann?"

"Fine, no symptoms... none that I can tell anyway."

"I didn't mean physically. How are you doing up here?" he tapped the side of his skull with his finger.

She sat back in her seat and cocked her head to one side. "Are you trying to psychoanalyze me, Paolio?"

"Hey... just talking to a friend." He gave a lopsided grin. "So how are you coping?"

"So far so good. I've only fallen over once and I've managed not to get anyone killed, yet—so that's a plus."

Paolo didn't reply. Instead he gave Jann a long look. Jann stayed quiet for a moment, examining the drink in her hand. "Well... if you really must know, ever since landing on the surface, I feel like a bit of a spare part. Like I'm just getting in the way."

"I see." Paolio took off his glasses, folded them and tucked them in the top pocket of his shirt. He sat back. "And why is that?"

Jann smiled. "See, you *are* analyzing me."

"Well, I have a soft spot for you. And it's as good a time as any. Here we are, two doctors having a chat on the surface of Mars." He spread his arms out and smiled.

"You're the doctor, Paolio. I have a doctorate in biology; it's not quite the same thing."

"You're right, it isn't. And that makes you probably the most important 'spare part' on this mission—right now." He leaned over and pointed out in the direction of Colony One. "We've just uncovered a dome full of biology out there, where we didn't think anything was still alive. No one planned for this. They all thought it was dead. Now we've got a really big puzzle to solve and I think you are the one that's going to play a vital part in solving it." He sat back again.

Jann thought about this as she fingered her drink. She looked out the HAB window at the night sky. "Yeah, no one saw this coming. I really hope I'm up to the task. I feel like there's a lot of responsibility thrust on me, that I hadn't planned for."

"Yes, well, sometimes we choose for ourselves and sometimes fate chooses for us, Jann."

"Like me being on this mission in the first place. I chose to enter the training program but, if Macallester hadn't dropped out at the last minute, well... I wouldn't be here, would I?"

"And how do you feel about that?"

"Unworthy, I suppose... I mean they selected me because I fit a profile, not because I was fully trained for the mission —and now, I just don't know."

"It seems they picked the right person, then."

Jann laughed. "Ha... we'll see. But somehow I don't get that impression from..." she didn't finish the sentence. She just sort of nodded at the sleeping commander."

"Ahhh... the Alphas."

"The what?"

"Alpha males, and females for that matter. It's not their job to like you, Jann. In fact they neither like nor dislike you. That's irrelevant to them."

"So you're saying I'm just being paranoid?"

"Is that the way you feel?"

Jann looked over at the canny doctor. She liked Paolio, felt comfortable around him. He was always there to talk to.

Still, she felt he was keeping an eye on her. Maybe that was a good thing.

"Is that the way you think I feel?"

He laughed. "Ah... you're getting wise to my ways, playing me at my own game." He looked down, like he was thinking, and then slowly leaned in across the table and spoke to her in a precise tone. "What I'm saying, Jann, is do not underestimate yourself. And do not let your perceptions of what other people think cloud your judgment."

Jann let this resonate in her mind. "Well, I generally don't. I just wish that..." she sighed.

"What?"

"That the commander, and Annis, would give me a goddamn break."

"Ahhh... so there it is," he sat back.

"They have their job to do, they *are* alphas. In any successful group there's always the leader who charges ahead and whips everyone else in to shape. But they are seldom the smartest, no?" He touched a finger to the side of his nose. "The smart ones are the ones you never expect, they're the ones still alive when everyone else is dead."

"Like whoever is still in that colony."

"Yes, exactly." He sat still for a moment looking out the HAB window, not that anything could be seen. "They're hiding from us, don't trust us, probably."

"Maybe they have a good reason."

"Perhaps—odd though." He stood up and went over to the coffee machine. "Sure you don't want one?"

"Oh, what the heck, okay. Just a small one. Not going to get any sleep now anyway."

Paolio fiddled with the machine as it hissed and spluttered. He brought the coffee back over to the table and presented it to Jann with all the flourish of a seasoned waiter in a Michelin starred restaurant.

"Et voila, Madam."

Jann sipped the astringent brew for a while. "You know Paolio, I actually applied for the Colony One Mars program, back in the day."

"Really? I did not know that."

"Nobody does. You're the first person I've ever told—outside of COM."

"You kept that very quiet."

"Yeah, I had this romantic notion of being part of the great colonization experiment, being in the vanguard of humans as an inter-planetary species."

"Didn't work out too well for them. Nothing romantic about suffocating to death on an alien world. So, tell me, what happened?"

"I got accepted into the ISA astronaut program around the same time. Seemed like a much better option."

"And you never told them?"

"God no. Didn't want them to think I was a flake of some

kind." She sat forward and took another sip of her coffee. "Sometimes, I think, in reality, it was me just copping out."

"What do you mean?"

"Well, let's face it, the possibility of me actually going to Mars by joining the ISA program was less than one percent. I knew that when I joined. I think it was just a way for me to dream but not actually commit."

"Well, here you are."

Jann looked around. "Yeah, be careful what you wish for. Because sometimes it might come true." She stood up. "I'm going to try and get some sleep. Big day tomorrow."

"For sure."

"Thanks... for the talk."

"My pleasure, Jann. Anytime. And remember, the difference between us and those colonists is we get to go home."

Jann turned around as she stepped on the plate elevator to ascend to the sleeping quarters. "Let's hope so, Paolio."

7

A NEW SOL

The discovery that the Colony One site was still functioning, at least technically, sent shock waves through ISA mission control back on Earth, not to mention the public media channels. Mars was now a twenty-four hour story with non-stop speculation and debate. All this was interspersed with an endless loop of archive footage of the early colonists, from liftoffs and interviews to daily life on the planet. The general consensus had always been that the colony had collapsed as a self-sustaining facility and that all fifty-four colonists were long dead. The brief for the current mission was simply one of survey and assessment of what was thought to be a derelict site. Not anymore, everything had changed.

. . .

COMMANDER DECKER WAS STILL LAID out in sick bay, and still unconscious. The rest of the crew had assembled in the operations area to review the overnight report in from mission control. The audio-visual on the main screen was that of ISA Mission Director summarizing their assessment of the discovery and advising on next actions.

"The top priority, as we see it, is to find whoever is still alive in the colony. If we can do that then we can get answers to all the other questions such as how did they survive, and why they didn't try to contact Earth. This is now a mission imperative." The ISA director droned on. *"Regarding Commander Decker, we understand that he is still unwell and as a precaution we strongly advise not breathing the air in the facility. Stay in your EVA suits at all times when surveying the site..."*

"That's bullshit," said Annis. "Everyone else is okay. We could get much more done by not having to bake in an EVA suit inside that place," she shook her head and sighed.

"...we are currently working with the COM people to get you as much data as we can on the ecosystem within the colony. But you have to realize that nobody thought we would ever need this information, so it's taking time to put together. In the meantime, we have sent you all the current data we have. As mission biologist, please have Dr. Jann Malbec review this data, it may prove useful..."

Jann had already downloaded the information sent overnight by ISA onto her tablet. She was quickly scrolling through it as she listened to the director. She sipped her second coffee of the morning, trying to wake herself up. She only had a few hours sleep the night before and was feeling it. The others seemed to be all fresh and alert, even Paolio. He was obviously made of stronger stuff than her.

The ISA Director droned on for a while but they were all losing interest and started to discuss the plan before the report ended.

"Okay, it's pretty clear what the objective is. Find whoever is still alive in there." The first officer, Annis Romanov, had assumed command since Decker was still incapacitated. "That means a full and thorough sweep of the entire facility. Every module, every compartment, every nook and cranny. I want no stone unturned."

"What about the commander?" said Lu.

"I'll stay here and keep an eye on him," said Paolio. He was refilling his coffee cup.

"No, Paolio, we'll need you at the site in case we find someone and have to assess their health. Anyway, the commander is out of danger, you said so yourself." Annis was being adamant.

"I'll stay," said Jann. "I need to go through all the data sent from mission control, so it's as good a time as any to do it." In reality she was seriously considering going back to bed when they all left.

"Okay, that's settled. Malbec will stay. Everyone else get ready to EVA in one hour."

. . .

THROUGH THE SMALL window in the HAB, Jann watched as the four crew marched across the Martian surface towards Colony One. She sat there for a time, watching them trail off into the distance. She wondered how long it would take to find the elusive colonists? And if they were found, then what? After a while she turned away from the window, sat down in the operations area and started studying the Colony One eco-system in earnest.

It soon became obvious to Jann that much of the information sent by the ISA was old and out of date. It was data that anyone with an interest in the Colony One Mars program could find out with a quick internet search. However, there were a number of interesting schematics of the facility. The one that caught her eye was the layout of the research laboratory. She studied it for a while and realized that there were a number of anomalies that she couldn't quite put her finger on.

Eventually, Jann got up and went over to the display table in operations and activated the current 3D map of the site. She brought up the schematic and zoomed in on the location of the research lab. On the charts that ISA had sent, it was a single module attached near to the biodome, at the functioning side of the colony. She flipped on the hi-res satellite image to overlay it on the schematic. The image now showed an additional large dome with four modules attached. This meant it had been greatly expanded at some point. It was now a major part of the facility. Perhaps this accounted for some of the missing modules, but not all of them. "I wonder what they were up to in there?" She switched off the display and went back to the reports.

Most of these were about plants that had been genetically modified specifically for the colony. Included was a group of reports which dealt with bacteria, genetically modified (GM) bacteria. The biggest stumbling block to the colonization of Mars was not water or oxygen, but soil. It was not possible to grow food crops in the Martian regolith as it contained a high concentration of perchlorates. Toxic to humans. At high doses it could cause thyroid problems. So it needed to be decontaminated first and this magic feat was performed by a genetically engineered bacterium. They converted the perchlorate into useful compounds including oxygen, and in the process cleaned up the soil so it could be used for food production. This was just one of the many GM bacteria in use in Colony One. But most of this information Jann knew already. There was nothing new in any of this. After a while fatigue got the better of her. She folded her arms on the table and slumped her head down. Within a few minutes, she had dozed off.

JANN AWOKE some time later to the sound of a low moan. She lifted her head up and listened intently. She heard it again. "Decker?" She couldn't see him from where she was sitting. He had been afforded some privacy in the small sick bay by virtue of a curtain. Jann stood up from the table and cautiously walked over to look in on him.

He was flat on his back, still out. *It must be eighteen hours now*, she thought. His breathing was normal, as far a she could tell, but his face had a pained contorted tightness. She leaned over to get a better look at his skin. His eyes flashed open. Jann stepped back in shock—not far enough. The commander grabbed her wrist in a viselike grip. She tried to twist free but he was too strong. His eyes were wide and wild. Then he spoke—just one word— "Contamination." He released his grip, his eyes closed, and he was still again.

"Holy shit." Jann rubbed her wrist and moved back against the wall of the HAB. "Robert?" She ventured a tentative step forward. "Commander, are you okay?" No answer. He was out for the count again. *Jesus, what was that about?* she thought as she stood there for a moment and considered what to do. *Contact Paolio, let him know.*

She hurried quietly back into the operations area, all the time trying to rub some feeling back into her wrist and keeping one eye on the commander. He didn't move again. She sat down at the communications desk and started thinking of what she was going to say, and how best to phrase it. She didn't want to sound like a frightened idiot. "Focus," she said to herself as she leaned into the desk to press the transmit button. She caught her reflection in the blank screen in front of her and thought she saw some other movement. She spun around, Decker was standing right behind her.

"Robert, you're awake."

He didn't reply, he had a vacant, glazed look in his eyes. He seemed confused as to where he was. He kept looking this way and that.

"Are you okay?"

"Contamination."

"What?" Jann was now backing away and putting some distance between herself and the commander—just in case. He advanced toward her. "I must get rid of this contamination."

"What are you talking about, what contamination?" Jann hadn't noticed at first but now she could see that he was carrying a heavy metal bar of some kind. He raised it over his head. Jann backed up, pressing herself against the HAB wall. "Robert, you're scaring the shit out of me. Put that down, put it down NOW!" She drove some authority into her voice and for a moment Decker stopped, like he was considering the situation. He looked at the tool briefly as if wondering what it was doing in his hand. Then he sprung forward and smashed it down, aiming for Jann's head. But she was too quick for him and darted out of the way as it clanged off the HAB wall.

"Robert... Christ, what are you doing?"

"You are a contaminant that must be eradicated."

Jann slid along the wall to put more space between them

and realized she was beside the airlock door. She opened it and dashed inside. But as she tried to shut the door the commander managed to get his arm inside, she couldn't close it. She pulled with all her might. Decker's arm swung about wildly and tried to grab her. It was no good. She couldn't get it closed—there was only one thing for it. She pushed open the door and swiveled a kick into Decker's stomach. He stumbled back and the bar fell out of his hand. She slammed the door shut and locked it.

Jann backed into a corner of the airlock. Her breathing was heavy. Adrenaline coursed through her body. She had never kicked anything other than a punching bag in her whole life. Part of her was concerned that she might have hurt the commander. No sound traveled through the airlock door. "Oh shit, what if I've injured him?" She had visions of Decker lying on the HAB floor, blood pouring from a head wound or some other injury he may have sustained as he fell. Still no sound.

Her breathing slowed and eventually she moved over to peer through the little window in the airlock door into the HAB. There was no sign of the commander. "Shit, what do I do now?" She could go back in and try to contain the deranged Decker. She could wait it out here until the crew returned, but that would be many hours from now. Or she could get out now—and run.

Jann hurriedly got into her EVA suit and started to depressurize the airlock. Before the sequence had completed, the commander's face appeared on the other side of the window. Jann was momentarily relieved that he was okay, before he started shouting. She couldn't hear. It looked like he was mouthing 'contamination.' Then he started bashing the door, over and over again. She could feel the force vibrating through the entire HAB.

"Come on... come on." The status light on the airlock finally illuminated green. Jann opened the outer door and jumped onto the planet's surface. She ran as fast as it was possible to run in a bulky EVA suit in one-third gravity. It wasn't beautiful, but it was probably a record.

She was quite a distance from the HAB when she realized she should have jammed something in the outer door so the commander couldn't get out. Once the airlock was repressurized, the door to the HAB would unlock. Would he come after her? Too late, she was not going back now. She kept on running.

8

JUST THE FEELING

The four ISA crew, led by Annis Romanov, had spent a number of hours investigating the deserted Colony One facility, searching systematically, ticking off areas as they went. Here and there lay the scattered evidence of recent activity: crumpled clothing, scraps from a half-eaten meal, food in the process of being stored—but no colonists. They also discovered areas that were not in use at all: sealed off, closed up, shut down. This was not surprising considering it was a facility designed for a hundred souls that now sustained just a few —somewhere.

Yet, their search was not completely in vain. It did pull back a veil on the mysterious Colony One survivors. It was evident that they were skilled at engineering. The crew found many areas with equipment being repaired or recycled, or in the process of being fashioned into something else.

After two hours of methodical investigation they reconvened in an area inside a small dome that looked to be a common room of some kind. It had worn and tattered seating. Crude drawings depicting Martian landscapes adorned the walls. It also had strange homemade furnishings and lighting that gave it a kind of scrapyard chic. It had the feeling of someone's home. But that someone had vanished, all that remained now was the feeling.

"There must be more to this base, a hidden section perhaps. Maybe some of the derelict areas are still functioning?" Annis had long given up on keeping herself cocooned inside an EVA suit, as had the others. They had become too hot and uncomfortable after the first half an hour inside the colony. So, one by one, they stripped off the bulky EVA suits down to basic flight-suit clothing.

"We've been everywhere, there's nowhere else to look. Nowhere that's got life support, that is." Lu sat down on one of the tatty armchairs. "It's obvious, they simply don't want to be found."

"But why? It doesn't make any sense. You'd think they would be jumping for joy at the prospect of being found alive after all this time." Paolio had joined her on another armchair. "Maybe they've been hiding for the last three years," he continued.

"What do you mean?" Annis was pacing.

"Think about it. The colony is presumed dead after the sandstorm, no message, no communication, not even an SOS scrawled in the sand outside, nothing. But someone is still alive, still living here—somewhere. Do you not think that's just a little weird?"

"And what about the others? There were... what... fifty-four colonists alive up here before the storm. There are six outside," ventured Lu.

"Seven. You forgot the one in the beehive hut," Kevin corrected.

"Okay seven. Then there's one, maybe two, hiding out here somewhere so that makes forty odd unaccounted for. No bodies, no EVA suits, so where are they?"

"Maybe they're compost, you know... recycled as plant food," said Kevin.

He was just about to sink his teeth into a colony apple when he stopped and thought better of it.

"All right, let's split up and see if we can find some better clues as to who's here. Paolio, take the medlab, Lu take the galley and accommodation modules. Kevin, I want you in the operations room and I'll do another sweep around the biodome. We'll meet back here in an hour."

"So what are we looking for this time?" Lu reluctantly got up from the armchair.

"Anything that will give us an idea of who's still here—and where they might be. Make a note of any computer terminals you come across. We can do a more forensic analysis later."

They all nodded and slowly wandered off to their appointed tasks.

THIS WAS Paolio's second time examining the medlab. The colony's sickbay, so to speak. It consisted of two connected modules, one of which was shut down, its door control panel dead. Conserving power, he assumed. He didn't find anything the first time so he was not expecting anything this time around. Mostly, he spent his time opening compartments and detailing the contents. It was well equipped and reasonably stocked with supplies of antibiotics, painkillers and a host of other medicines.

It was very quiet, dimly lit, and just a little creepy. Every now and again some machine deep within the bowels of the colony would start up and Paolio would get a jolt. On more than one occasion, he could feel his heart race as some eerie feeling got the better of his rationality.

"Anything?"

He jumped. "Jesus Lu, don't sneak up on me like that."

"Sorry, didn't mean to give you a fright."

"Nothing here. Weird isn't it? It's like the Mary Celeste."

"What's that?"

"It was the name of an old sailing ship found abandoned off the Azores, back in the late eighteen hundreds."

"Never heard of it," replied Lu.

"The thing is, when they boarded the ves completely deserted. But there were plates on the galley table, like someone had just eaten. Yet, they searched it top to bottom and found no one. It's still a mystery to this day."

"I see what you mean."

"Anyway, I thought you were supposed to be searching the galley?"

"Eh... just didn't want to be on my own."

"I know how you feel."

"Funny, isn't it? We spent all those months cooped up on the Odyssey, getting in each other's space and now... well I get freaked out if I'm alone," she moved closer to Paolio.

"It's perfectly natural to get a bit freaked out in this place." He waved an arm around. Lu came closer still and started to shake. Paolio embraced her. "Hey, it's okay." She held him tight and he could feel her heart beat against his chest. She tipped her head back, gave him a long look and then kissed him.

"Paolio." The voice of First Officer Annis Romanov squawked in his headset. *"I just got a message from the commander, he's awake. But we have a problem."*

"Shit." Paolio pulled his head away.

"What is it?" said Lu.

"It's Annis." He tapped his earpiece. "Decker is awake."

"Can't you just ignore it?"

"No, I can't. There's a problem." He pressed his earpiece again. "Annis, yes. How is he?"

"He's fine, a slight headache, that's all. But it seems Malbec has gone AWOL."

"Jann? What happened?"

"He says when he woke up the HAB was deserted, didn't know what was going on. I explained to him we left Malbec there to keep an eye on things, but she's gone and her EVA suit's gone too. You better go talk to him—and meet us in the common room right away."

"Okay."

"What is it?" Lu looked anxious.

"Jann's gone missing. Come on, Annis wants us in the common room." Paolio tapped his earpiece again, but this time to contact Decker.

"Commander, this is Dr. Corelli."

"Doctor, go ahead."

"How are you feeling?"

"Fine, feel great actually. But I got a bit of a scare when there was no one here."

"Where's Dr. Malbec?"

"No idea, the HAB was empty when I woke up. Look, I'm heading over to the colony. I'll talk to you there."

"Are you sure you're physically up to it?"

"Yes, fine. We need to find Malbec, though."

"Okay, we'll see you here." Paolio was concerned for Jann. She didn't strike him from their conversation the previous night as someone ready to abdicate responsibility. Then again, he wasn't sure he knew what the hell was going on anymore.

THE OTHERS HAD ASSEMBLED in the common room by the time Paolio and Lu arrived.

"I knew she wasn't ready for this mission. I don't know why they picked her in the first place, she's a liability." Annis was waving her hands in the air, pacing up and down.

"Have you tried to contact her? If she's gone EVA she should have her comms on."

"Tried that, no joy, nothing."

"The commander is on his way," said Paolio. "Let's just stay calm and try to find her."

They all turned as they heard a sound from the airlock; it was depressurizing. "Decker?" said Kevin.

"No, he was just leaving the HAB, it's too soon," said Paolio.

"Maybe it's a colonist?" said Lu.

They looked from one to the other and waited. The outer door opened and someone entered, the door closed and the airlock began to pressurize again. The green alert flashed, the door swung open and out stepped Jann Malbec. She collapsed to her knees on the floor. Paolio rushed over and helped her remove her helmet. She was sweating and breathing hard. "Jann, what the hell is going on?" She struggled to get her breathing under control as she spoke.

"The commander, he's gone crazy, attacked me with a metal bar or something, tried to bash my head in, I had to escape, run, talking crazy shit, contamination." She put her head in her hands and shook. They looked blankly at her. Annis knelt down beside her putting her hand on Jann's shoulder. "We've just been talking to Decker and he's perfectly okay, nothing crazy about him."

Jann's eyes widened and she backed away from Annis. "No, seriously, he's crazy, dangerous."

"He didn't sound that way to me, Jann," said Paolio. "What the hell happened in the HAB?"

"I told you."

"Tell us again, from the top."

Jann regained some composure. "He woke up suddenly, grabbed my wrist and said something about 'contamination,' then conked out again. I went over to the comms desk to call you and he was standing behind me, looking crazy. Then he attacked me, with a metal bar, I think. I barricaded myself in the airlock. He was trying to bash the door down so I got into my EVA suit and ran here. That's it."

Annis stood up. "Hmmm, well he sounded totally rational to me. He's on his way over now."

"What? No, you can't let him in, no way."

"Calm down, don't get hysterical, get a grip," said Annis.

Jann stood up with the help of Paolio and Lu. She looked

at him, pleading. "I'm not going crazy, it happened like I said."

"It's okay, Jann, no one's saying you're crazy."

The airlock light flashed red, it was depressurizing again. Decker had arrived. Jann moved away from the entrance and behind a workbench. "Paolio, stay with her, keep her calm, don't let her go crazy."

"I'm not goddamn crazy."

He moved over to where Jann was standing and watched her closely. "Just stay cool, Jann."

The door opened and the commander walked in. He took off his helmet and looked over at Jann. "So you showed up finally. Where did you get to?"

Jann said nothing. She just stood wide eyed.

"How are you feeling Robert?" said Paolio.

"Fine, although I'd be better if I knew what the hell was going on."

"What do you remember?"

"I remember waking up alone." He walked towards Jann. "Where did you get to, you were supposed to be keeping an eye on me."

Jann backed up. "Don't come near me... stay away." She grabbed a knife off the workbench.

"Woah... easy now Malbec, put that down, we don't want anybody getting hurt."

"Just stay away."

Paolio moved over to where he left his doctor's bag beside

the airlock entrance. From it he took a syringe with 5cc of cyclophromazine. It was small enough to conceal in his hand. He moved back towards Jann, and while she was distracted fending off the commander, he slipped in behind her and jabbed her in the neck. Paolio grabbed her around the waist as she collapsed, unconscious.

"Jesus Christ, she's gone nuts, this is all we need," said Annis.

"Can someone please tell me what the hell is going on?"

"Lu, help me get her into the medlab." Between them they carried her in and laid her on the bed. Paolio checked her vitals. "She'll be out for a few hours."

"What happened to her?" said Lu as she brushed the hair from Jann's face.

"I don't know, I really don't," he shook his head a few times.

Once he was satisfied that she was okay, they returned to the common room. Annis was in the process of explaining to Decker what had happened.

"It makes no sense," said Decker. He looked over at Paolio. "What do you think?" Paolio didn't know what to think. He was glad that the commander seemed well again but now this breakdown of Jann's was a major concern. "She'll be out for a few hours. I can try and make an assessment of her mental health once she wakes up. But even if she seems fine we'll have to keep a very close eye on her."

"I'll not have her mess up this mission, it's too important.

Christ, this is all we need." He was rubbing his head. "Speaking of which, have you found anything?"

"Nothing, at least no colonists. We've searched everywhere we could. We found lots of evidence of recent activity, by at least one person. But where they are is still a mystery," said Annis.

"There are still quite a number of areas in the colony that are intact but shut down. So maybe that's the next place to look," offered Kevin.

"Show me where we've searched so far and what's left."

"Sure." Kevin produced a tablet and laid it flat on the common room table. He activated it and a 3D schematic of the Colony One site ballooned out across the table surface. "All these areas here in green we've searched. The ones in red I've identified as derelict. Probably structurally dangerous. We'll need to be careful entering any of those areas. All these areas here are offline but still intact, as far as I can tell. They're shut down, no power or life support."

"What's this area here, looks pretty big." Decker was pointing to a small dome with a number of modules attached at the other end of the main biodome.

"Research lab."

"Might be worth getting in there and having a look around."

"Tricky."

"Why's that?"

"There's no outer airlock so we can't just EVA in there. We'd have to power it up and pressurize it first."

"I see." The commander rubbed his head again. "Annis, what does mission control know?"

"That the place is not dead and that you are feeling ill."

"You need to send them an update on what we've found so far. And let them know I'm fine now. We'll keep quiet about Malbec for the moment, okay? I don't want them getting too concerned."

"Will do."

He breathed a sigh and rubbed his head again.

"Are you all right?" said Paolio.

"Yeah, just a bit of a headache."

"I'll get you something for it."

"That would be great, thanks."

"So what's our next move here?" said Kevin.

The commander thought about this for a moment. "We assess the infrastructure, find out what's working, how it works and what resources are available. We'll do a complete inventory on all Colony One systems."

"That's probably going to take weeks to do."

"Well you guys better get to it. Me, I'm actually going to lie down for a little while, I feel a bit woozy."

"You're still not a hundred percent, Robert. Come, I'll show you where there's an accommodation pod, you can rest there," said Annis.

"I'm just going to check on Jann," said Paolio. "Lu, do you want to join me?"

"Eh... I need to get back to checking the galley again." She gave a little shrug of her shoulders.

"Okay." Paolio headed back into the medlab and looked down at the unconscious figure of Dr. Jann Malbec. "Well Jann, you sure as hell know how to ruin a person's day."

9

COM

Peter VanHoff scanned the report from First Officer Annis Romanov. It was brief, yet interesting in that it was from her and not Commander Decker. Nonetheless, it seemed that he had recovered from his mystery illness, which was a major relief. Still, Peter could not help feeling a certain unease that the commander was not fully operational, so to speak. His uneasiness stemmed from memories of the mayhem that preceded the demise of Colony One. The final communications from the stricken outpost spoke of a deep psychosis affecting a number of colonists. Ever since, the question in many people's minds had been: was it this that caused the destruction of Colony One and not the sandstorm? The question, of course, was still unanswered.

He put the report aside and pulled up the site schematic

that the first officer had sent. A good deal of Colony One was still intact, including the research lab. This was a section of the facility that he was acutely interested in. Nevertheless, if the lab were to be brought back online, how much of the scientific data would realistically still be viable? It was a question that greatly occupied VanHoff.

Shortly before Colony One went dark, the scientists working there hinted at a major genetic breakthrough. But the data was never transmitted as the colony started to come apart at the seams. So he had all but given up on acquiring this information. Now though, it seemed he had been given a second chance. But it was a double edged sword, he needed to be careful. What went on in that research lab was for COM eyes only. It would be very damaging for them should it become public knowledge.

VanHoff looked at his watch, time for the board to convene. Who could he trust? Initially he had considered that Rick Mannersman might be a problem. But the media frenzy surrounding the discovery was keeping him very busy —at the center of attention. The fact that Mannersman was motivated simply by greed and self-aggrandizement meant he was relatively easy to manipulate, as long as he was distracted. Most of the others were inconsequential and easy to handle. But could they be relied on if tough decisions were required?

Leon Maximus, on the other hand, Peter admired. He was motivated by a seemingly sincere desire to advance human civilization. To make it an interplanetary species. To establish a Planet B, as he liked to call it. He was a rare breed indeed. None of this would have been possible if were not for him and his genius. His company had developed the rocket technology to get the first colonists to Mars. Still, it was a slow tedious process. It was an eight month trip and, with the way the planets orbited each other, a tight two year launch window.

In the end, it was Leon's near maniacal insistence on the research and development of an exotic device known as an EM Drive that changed the numbers. A bizarre contraption that defied normal engineering convention. As far as Peter understood, it was essentially a microwave in a cone shaped box. How it worked nobody could really explain to him without delving in to the realms of quantum physics. Ultimately, it was an extraordinary breakthrough. Here was a simple engine, with no moving parts, not subjected to enormous forces, that worked simply by electricity. With enough solar panels strapped to your spaceship you could have thrust on tap any time you wanted. Swap the solar panels with a small nuclear reactor and all of a sudden space became a much smaller place.

This radically changed the nature of a mission to Mars and ultimately the economics of Colony One. The journey time went from over eight months to just under seventy days. Now more missions could be sent: more supplies, more equipment, more colonists. And, coupled with Leon's inspired reusable main stage design, it came in at a fraction of the initial cost.

Nonetheless, after a few short years and twenty odd colonists later, the excitement was beginning to fade and COM was finding it hard to generate revenue from the media rights alone. This was when Peter VanHoff entered the scene. But he was not interested in some grand vision for humanity. That, he left to the dreamers. No, it was his passion for genetic research and his quest to crack the complex process of aging that involved him in the COM consortium. He realized early on that there were things one could do on Mars that were simply not ethically possible on Earth. Particularly in the area of xeno-combinant genetic research and genome manipulation. And, as a bonus, there were a great many corporations willing to pay good money for the ability to do this, far from the prying eyes of legal scrutiny. So he convinced Leon Maximus and the others in COM of the opportunity for building such a biotech research facility. With failing media revenues due to faltering public interest, they had really no other option. They bought into it and Peter VanHoff took effective control of COM.

HE PUT THE REPORT AWAY, stood and looked out across the snow capped mountains in the distance. His mind considered the implications of this report from Romanov. It was full with possibility, uncertainty and not a little danger.

They would need to tread carefully. He shook his head and walked back into his study and touched the controls on the holo-tablet. A small illuminated screen materialized in midair, less than an arm's reach in front of him. It moved as he moved. He reached out and touched a virtual icon on the screen. Several avatar symbols appeared and floated in the space before him, one for each member of the board. They arrayed themselves around Peter VanHoff's field of vision like dead relatives in a Victorian séance. The meeting was about to begin.

"Good evening gentlemen." There was a collective murmuring of greetings and acknowledgments as the ghostly figures moved and shifted in the space before him. Peter VanHoff continued. "You all know by now that the crew of the ISA Mars mission have successfully landed on the planet's surface—and that the colony is not as dead as we thought." This was met with various nods and grunts from the avatars representing the board members of the Colony One Mars consortium.

"To recap, the ISA crew entered the colony facility to discover that it is still functioning and there is possibly at least one survivor. To facilitate a more comprehensive search they removed their helmets and operated wholly within the colony environment. A short while later Commander Decker became ill."

"What? Why did nobody warn them?" it was Rick Mannersman who voiced this concern.

Peter ignored it and continued. "According to First Officer Annis Romanov's latest report the commander has made a full recovery."

"But what if it's happening again?"

"We don't know that yet, so let's just stick to the facts," insisted Peter.

"What about the research lab?"

"Ah, the lab, yes. Well it's still intact, although not online." With that, there was a general air of excitement within the group.

"I'm sure you'll appreciate that there is eh... sensitive information in that laboratory that is not for public consumption."

"I knew we shouldn't have got into bed with ISA. If they were to get an inkling of the research that went on up there then there would be all hell to pay," said Mannersman. His avatar bobbed and bristled as he spoke.

"Well they're not."

"How can you be so sure?"

"Because we have our own agent on site, remember? So they can see to it that it does not fall into the wrong hands. Furthermore, we now have an incredible opportunity to return this research to Earth."

The avatars shifted and murmured. They were all salivating at this prospect.

"Do you really think it still exists?"

"If the information we have received is correct then there

is every possibility that the... eh, Analogue is intact." It was Nagle who responded. As the COM member assigned to ISA mission control he was in a unique position to validate all expedition data.

"We are moving our own satellite back into position over the Colony One site and running full communications diagnostics on it as we speak. Assuming our agent performs their duties then we will soon know if what we seek is indeed viable."

"I trust I don't need to remind you all of what this will mean to the future of humanity, if we succeed." Peter decided to up the ante.

"You're all forgetting one major issue. What if it's happening again? What if the unfortunate Commander Decker is succumbing to the same malaise that brought the colony down in the first place?" said Mannersman.

"You don't know that for sure."

"You're right, I don't. But if it *is* happening again, then this may be the last we hear from the crew of the ISA Mars mission."

10

MEDLAB

Paolio wandered into the medlab to check on Jann. What happened to her? he wondered. What made her flip like that? There had been no indication the previous night. She was a little anxious perhaps—but then again, that was understandable considering the circumstances. He thought back to the time they spent on the Odyssey en route to Mars. There had been no sign then either, at least none that he could discern. Nothing to indicate Malbec's potential mental frailty.

Another issue was the commander. Paolio was still not convinced that Decker had fully recovered, although outwardly he seemed remarkably alert. He had given him something for the headache and he was now resting in one of the accommodation modules. This concerned the doctor, considering the commander had just spent eighteen hours asleep.

As for the others, Lu had gone back to doing a search of the galley and accommodation modules. He would check in on her later. Kevin, the mission engineer, had ensconced himself in the operations area, a section of Colony One given over to control systems. He was busy trying to get a sense of how the colony functioned: power supply, environmental controls, life support. Romanov had gone off to file a report to mission control. They would be pleased to hear that the commander was on the mend. But they were still no further along in the search for the survivors. With Jann now a concern, it seemed to Paolio that bit by bit, little by little, the mission was losing its way.

HE SPENT some time checking Jann's vitals. She looked comfortable enough even though she was still encased in her EVA suit. Paolio had considered stripping it off and taking her out of it, he didn't want her to overheat. But she would be awake in a while so he just removed her boots and gloves, pushed a pillow under her head, and left it at that. He stood back from his handiwork and surveyed the rest of the medlab module. It was in fact two modules connected together. But only one of them was operational. He walked to the far end and checked the door into the disused section.

The control panel was dead. He fiddled with it for a while but it was pretty obvious it was never going to open, not without power. There were quite a number of these areas in the colony: shut down, offline, disused. They would soon have to start investigating them. But not before they had a better understanding of the colony control systems.

Along one wall of the medlab were a number of terminals. Paolio swiped a hand over one of the control interfaces—no joy. He hunted around the workbench looking for a power source. Eventually he found a bank of switches that looked like they might control power. He flicked one marked 'terminals' and the area illuminated followed by a number of beeps. He waved his hand over the control interface again and this time it came to life and rendered a 3D animated COM logo just above its surface. He touched the logo and it split up into a myriad of icons for programs and files. What he really wanted to find were medical records. Something to shed a little more light on the colonists that lived here. It might give him an idea of what happened to them in those last desperate days.

Paolio had always been of the opinion that there was more to the demise of Colony One than just the sandstorm. The last communication from Nills Langthorp had intimated at deeper psychological issues affecting the colonists. Perhaps this had hindered their ability to maintain sustainable life support? Yet it was never discussed within

COM, or the ISA for that matter. Any mention of this line of enquiry was quickly dismissed as unnecessary speculation. Nevertheless, it had always been in the back of his mind. He wondered if this was the same illness that had afflicted the commander. He dared not mention his concerns to the others, in case he raised the paranoia levels unnecessarily.

Then there was Jann. Was she also affected? He put that thought out of his mind and went back to studying the terminal. He touched on various icons looking for anything that might help shed some light on the mysteries of Colony One. After a short time he finally came to a gallery of colonists. There was a headshot for each, tagged with a cryptic alphanumeric reference. He was about to touch one to open it when he heard a series of screams emanating from deep within the bowels of the colony. He jumped up from the terminal. "Lu!"

Paolio ran out of the medlab heading for the galley to check on Lu. He frantically searched to no avail. "Lu?" he shouted. No answer. "Damn where is she?" He moved out of the galley and into the main workshop. "Lu, are you there?" Still no answer. He turned around and about five meters behind him stood Commander Decker. He had a vacant expression and seemed to be looking up somewhere towards the ceiling. Paolio took a tentative step forward. "Commander, are you okay? Did you hear that scream, have you seen Lu?" Decker didn't reply. He fixed his gaze on Paolio with an intense, questioning look. Paolio was about to move towards the commander when he realized Decker was holding a long steel bar. Its end was covered in blood, some of which was dripping onto the floor. "Jesus, Robert. What's going on?"

Decker slowly raised the bar. Paolio backed away. Decker lunged. He was too quick for the doctor and struck him square across the shoulder—with force. "Contamination. It must be eradicated."

Paolio heard his collarbone snap as white-hot pain rifled up his neck and into his brain. The second blow connected with the side of Paolio's head. He lost his balance and went flying over a pile of workshop junk, landing hard on the floor and banging into the side of a tall rack. It rocked and tottered and finally came crashing down on top of his leg. He heard the snap and more pain than Paolio had ever known in his life coursed through his body. He cursed and screamed and looked around to try and see where Decker was. But the area was now dark. "Has the power gone?" Paolio couldn't move, he waited for Decker to come and attack him again—but he didn't. Had he moved off somewhere else? It was deathly quiet.

Paolio tried to get some control of his mind and calm himself down. His body screamed with pain, his head throbbed and his vision was blurry. With his good arm, he managed to drag himself backwards into a corner and hide. It was all he could do. It was very dark. He was sure the power must be out. Then he heard it. Another scream, and another, and then silence. "Lu, no, not Lu." He couldn't bear the pain, it was too much. Then he saw a muddy pool of his own blood seeping out from under him. The break in his leg must be bad, very bad. He was a doctor so he knew what happened next—he was bleeding to death. His vision began to dim, his thoughts dulled and his eyes slowly closed.

11

COLD, SO COLD

Jann's eyes snapped open. It was cold, her breath condensed and she shivered even though she was still in her EVA suit. She sat up and looked around. Her gloves and helmet were on a bench on the far side of the medlab. There was no sign of anyone. Then she remembered what had happened. She had really lost the plot, freaking out like that and waving a knife around. Could she really blame Paolio for what he did? Too late anyway, the damage was done. Now she would be regarded as the *crazy one*.

"Hello, anyone there?" No answer. *There's no power*, she thought, must *be why it's so cold. Where is everybody?*

She swung her legs over the side of the bed and stood up. She was a little shaky and took a few moments to find her balance. The light in the lab was dim, but she could still see well enough. What time was it? How long had she been out? Jann made her way over to the bench, took her gloves and helmet and put them on, just in case. If there was some emergency she could get life support from the suit almost instantly. Probably a good idea. She strapped on her boots but left the visor on her helmet open.

She stood in the medlab for a few moments considering what to do next. Silence. Cold, dark silence. Not a sound. She listened; not even the pervasive low hum that comes with space travel, an inevitable consequence of the need to be permanently encased in life support. The hum that you only notice when it's gone. Maybe they're trying to restore power? But then, why didn't Paolio, or anyone, stay here for when I woke up? "Hello?" she ventured into her helmet comm. "Malbec here, anybody please respond..." Nothing. Maybe she should go look for them. Or maybe she should get out and make for the HAB. She checked the time; there was still another hour or so of daylight left. But the Martian night came quick. It would be pitch black out on the surface, no moon to illuminate the way. She did have the HAB beacon so she could follow that if necessary and her helmet had a powerful floodlight. Jann thought about arming herself with a weapon of some kind. A baseball bat would be good, or a knife. Then again, maybe not. It didn't work out too well the last time she tried that. So she left it, no point in exacerbating the situation.

After deliberating her options for some time, Jann cautiously moved out of the medlab and into the main common area. Pale daylight filtered down through the domed roof, enough to illuminate her way. "Hello?" she listened. Nothing. "Where the hell are they?" She jumped as she heard a cracking sound from high up in the dome superstructure; it was adjusting to the change in temperature. Metal contracting and shifting causing a creaking that echoed around the facility. Jann made her way towards the biodome, all the time looking around for anything that might give her a clue as to the whereabouts of the crew.

She stopped at the entrance of the short tunnel that led to the biodome. Ahead of her, she could make out a crewmember sitting on the floor, their back resting against the tunnel wall. "Hello?" They didn't respond; she moved closer. It was Lu. Her head was covered in blood from a serious gash on her skull. Her eyes were wide—and dead. "Lu, Jesus... Lu!" Jann rushed to her, removed one of her gloves and checked Lu's pulse. Nothing. She slumped down onto the floor opposite the lifeless Lu Chan, and cried for the loss of her friend. "Lu, what happened?" But Lu had nothing to say.

SOMETHING FAST MOVED between the rows of vegetation inside the biodome. Jann caught a fleeting glimpse in the corner of her eye and she froze. It moved again. She stood up slowly, keeping her back to the tunnel wall and moved in through the entrance to investigate. It came at her like a freight train and something heavy hit her hard on the side of her head. The force knocked her forward and she went careening over a grow bed and crashed to the ground on the other side. Her suit helmet had taken the blow and held, otherwise she would be dead, or dying. She rolled over onto her back. Commander Decker towered over her. He stood motionless, glaring down at her with a demonic stare. She lifted herself up on her elbows and tried to shuffle backwards. She was dizzy from the blow. "Decker, what the hell?" He stopped and tilted his head slightly to one side like he was considering her. He then looked over at the grow-bed, pulled a long sharp metal stake out of the ground and hefted it like a spear. He advanced. Jann frantically kicked out but it was a futile action. He raised the spear, aiming to skewer her through the abdomen. Jann screamed and held her arms out in a last desperate act of self-preservation.

From nowhere, Kevin Novack appeared and struck the commander across the back of the head with a heavy bar. Decker reeled and lost his balance. The engineer hit him again, this time on his shoulder, and Decker went flying over a grow-bed and collapsed on the floor. He stayed still. Kevin looked at the prostrate commander, ready to strike again. Satisfied that he wasn't moving he reached down to help Jann up.

"You okay?"

"I told you he was deranged."

"I know, I know... you were right, what can I say?"

"What happened?"

"He was perfectly fine then he started talking crazy. Lu tried to talk to him, and he just... killed her. I couldn't get to her in time. Then he ran off. I've been stalking him since."

"What about the others? Paolio?"

"I don't know, it all happened so fast. I don't know where they are."

"Hello, Malbec here. Paolio, Annis... please respond?" Jann spoke in her comm. Nothing. "Is no one wearing a headset?"

Kevin shrugged. "I took mine off in the operations area."

"How long has the power been out?"

"Shortly after Decker went crazy."

"Shit, look..."

She pointed at the spot where the commander had been —he was gone.

"Come on, let's get out of here... now!" Kevin grabbed Jann and moved her towards the tunnel exit. He pushed her through the door and then started to close it. It was stiff.

"Shit, give me a hand, Jann, we can close him in here if we get this shut." The short tunnel between the main biodome and the common area was designed as an airlock so each section could be sealed off. But the doors had been rigged to stay open. Jann had just turned back to help when

Kevin's eyes went wide and a large dark bloodstain spread across his abdomen. A metal spear protruded from its center. He dropped to his knees. "Kevin... no..."

Decker stood behind the stricken Novack holding the bloodied metal shaft. He looked at it with a vacant curiosity, like it was something alien. He seemed mesmerized by it. Jann backed slowly down the short tunnel. She grabbed the door at the far end and put all her weight behind it. It moved, but slowly. It was stiff and needed all her strength to operate. Decker's head jerked up as he noticed the swinging door. He shot forward with frightening speed. But Jann had her shoulder to the heavy door—it was gaining momentum and clicked closed just as Decker crashed into it. She bounced off it with the force and slid across the floor, but the door held. She rushed back and spun the locking wheel, grabbed a bar from one of the scrap piles and wedged it into the handle. Just in time. She could see it rattle as the commander tried to open it. He stopped and for a brief moment silence returned to the colony. Then there was a massive crash as the door shook, and another, and another. He was throwing himself against it in a crazed frenzy. The entire facility resonated with the force, but the door held. Jann backed away.

The banging stopped. Jann wasn't sure if that was a good thing. It probably was, but now she didn't know what he was up to. The daylight was also fading fast. She needed to get out now and make a run for the HAB. Like she did this morning, running from the demented Decker.

She was about to flip her visor down and make for the airlock when she heard a low moan. She froze. It came from over by the workshop. There it was again. She picked up a heavy metal rod from one of the scrap tables and cautiously headed towards the sound. She kept low, moved behind a mound of disassembled machines and peered in. On the floor, in a gap between a row of storage boxes, she saw a pair of bloodied legs. She shifted closer to get a better view. The legs were attached to Dr. Paolio Corelli. He was sitting on the floor with his back resting against the dome wall, hiding as best he could. "Paolio."

His face was bloodied but he was still alive, still breathing. She shook his shoulder. "Paolio, it's me Jann." His eyes opened slowly. "Jann." He coughed and spat a bloody gob on the floor. She crouched down beside him. "Paolio, can you move?"

"My leg... broken, collar bone... ribs I think."

"Decker is trapped in the biodome, for the moment. We need to get out of here."

He grabbed her by the arm and pulled her closer. "Lu... where's Lu?"

"She's... dead, Paolio... so is Kevin. I don't know about Annis.

Paolio let out a long, gut-wrenching moan. "No... not Lu." Then he let go of her and slumped back. "I'm sorry, Jann. I screwed up... thought you had gone off the rails." He spat again.

"It's okay. You probably saved my life, Paolio. If I wasn't out for the count I might be dead by now. Come on." She put her arm under his and tried to help him up.

"Ahhhhh..." he collapsed again. "It's no use, I'm too broken."

"Don't give up on me now, just get your shit together." She raised her voice and put some sting into it. Anything to get him to move. "We've got to try and get to the HAB. If you can get outside I can call the mule and you can ride it there. You've got to try."

"Okay..." He steeled himself and, with Jann's help, managed to stand up on one leg. He was weak and unstable, but seemed to revive a little now that he was upright and had purpose.

"Where's your EVA suit and helmet?"

Paolio rubbed his head as he balanced himself against the wall. "Over by the airlock... I think."

Jann put his arm over her shoulder and propped him up. "Okay, ready?" He nodded, and they shuffled off. Paolio hopped on one leg, he could put no weight on the other. They made slow progress.

"Hold it... I've got to stop. Oh god, I'm a total mess." He balanced himself against a workbench, breathing hard and looking deathly pale. "I don't think I can make it."

"Yes you can, just keep going, come on."

"Jann, I'm a doctor, I know the story. I'm losing a lot of

blood. I've already passed out once. Unless I get it stopped soon, I'll bleed to death. I'm screwed, Jann."

It was clear to her that Paolio had a point. Their only option now was to head for the medlab and take their chances.

"The medlab then. You can make it that far. Come on."

"No Jann. Every thing's gone to rat shit, leave me, get out of here, get off this planet... do you hear me? Get off while you still can... go now."

"I'm not leaving you here, you can forget that idea. And I'm not leaving Annis either." She threw his arm around her shoulders and hoisted him up.

"She may be dead too, Jann."

"Move, we're wasting time."

JANN HELPED him onto the bed in the medlab and rushed back to shut the door. She needed to find something to wedge into the closing mechanism but time was running out for Paolio, so she left it and went back to him. His leg looked bad. His flight suit was saturated with blood. "I'm going to have to cut this off." She hunted around for some surgical instruments and found several trays. She grabbed a set of cutters, probably designed for this exact job. She surveyed Paolio's leg more closely. He had managed to apply a tourniquet to his upper leg just above the knee. Best not touch that for the moment.

"Are you sure you want me to do this?"

"My leg's not much good to me if I'm dead."

"Okay." She started cutting. It didn't take long to reveal the wound and to realize that it was worse than she thought. He had a large gash on the inside left calf, and the bone protruded from a gelatinous mass of blood. "Oh shit." She hadn't meant to alarm him, it just escaped out of her mouth. Paolio lifted himself up on one elbow and assessed the damage to his body. "Shit." He collapsed back down again.

She found some gauze and started cleaning around the wound. Paolio groaned in pain. "Stop. Jann. Wait." He raised himself up again and this time took a longer look at the wound. The bleeding seemed to have stopped, which was something at least. But he knew the score, what he wanted Jann to do next would either save him or kill him. It was fifty-fifty, at best.

"Jann, listen to me. Here's what I want you to do..." before he could finish they heard an intense banging from across the dome. Jann ran to the lab door and looked out. Decker was trying to get the main biodome door opened. She could see the bar she used to wedge it closed was working itself loose with the vibration. They didn't have much time.

"Jann!"

She shut the medlab door and this time jammed a long, hardened steel surgical instrument in to the locking mechanism. It would buy them time, nothing more.

"Jann!"

"Paolio, Decker's breaking his way out of the biodome."

"Jann, listen to me, listen to me."

She stopped. "Sure Paolio."

"I want you to reset the bone and stitch me up."

"Are you serious?"

He grabbed her arm and brought her face closer to his, and gritted his teeth. "Do it. Do it now before I change my mind."

"Okay, okay. I'll need to find some clean bandages first." He released her arm and sunk back down on the bed. Jann backed off and started opening drawers and doors and pulling out everything she could find. She knew what he was asking. Resetting the bone would mean starting the bleeding again, as well as the excruciating agony. He might just pass out from the pain... if he was lucky. She found some bandages, still packaged so still sterile, if that actually mattered in the rarefied Colony One environment. There was loud crash outside. Decker was out of the biodome. She ran back to Paolio. *If there was ever a time to get focused this is it. Do it now*, she thought.

"Paolio, ready?"

"No," he sighed. "Yes, yes." He managed a hint of a smile.

She surveyed the wound as best she could, but there was no easy way to do this. She placed one hand gently on his leg just below the knee. Paolio screamed. She whipped her hand away, Paolio held his forehead and moaned. "Here, bite down on this." She pushed a plastic handled instrument between his teeth, not that it was going to do much good, it was more psychological. She readied herself at the foot of the bed to reset the bone. "Ready in three." Paolio groaned and nodded. She grabbed his calf just above the ankle. "One... " and jerked it back with a twist. Paolio screamed in agony. The bone retracted back in through the open wound. She could feel it grind around inside as she tried to feel it back into place. Paolio raged and roared and she was sure he was going to pass out. Blood oozed out of the wound and pooled all around, it dripped on to the floor and her hands were wet and slippery. She couldn't do this to him any more, when she felt it was right she stopped. "I think that's it." Paolio didn't respond. She quickly wrapped his leg with a tight bandage to close the wound. It wasn't pretty, but they were way beyond that now. She finished the bandage and the blood flow had lessened. He looked deathly white, his body drenched in sweat and his breathing shallow. *He's still alive,* she thought, *but for how much longer? I've probably just killed him.*

She sunk down on to the cold floor of the lab and cradled her head in her hands, rocking back and forth, like some long-term inmate of a desolate gulag whose mind had been eroded by eternal hopelessness. How did everything get so messed up so quickly? Lu and Kevin were dead. Killed by the unhinged Decker, and Paolio, what hope was there for him now? Annis was probably dead as well. Soon, there would be just her.

Even if she were to run now there was no way out. She wasn't going to leave Paolio. And there was no way she could get him into an EVA suit before Decker got out. They were stuck here. What's more, with no power in the colony it was only a matter of time before the air became so saturated with CO2 it would be poisonous. How long, she had no idea. Hours, days, weeks? It didn't matter; Decker would get them long before that.

But there was no respite, the lab shook and reverberated as Decker tried to get in. She jumped up, "Shit," and backed away as the door rocked again. There was nothing for it; she would have to make a stand—here, in this lab, on this desolate planet. It would be her end and she knew it. Jann swept the lab with the light from her helmet in search of anything she could use as a weapon. The door reverberated again. She picked up a long, sharp surgical knife and held it with both hands out in front of her. She hoped to God it would not be the instrument of her own death. Her body shook and sweat streamed down her face, stinging her eyes. She could smell her own fear. *Hold fast old girl,* she thought, *focus.*

The banging stopped and Jann entered a twilight zone of the unknown. At least with the noise she knew where he was. Once it stopped her anxiety ratcheted up, notch by notch, as she waited for the inevitable onslaught of the crazed commander. She held fast.

Time passed and the light from her helmet grew dim, soon she would see nothing but total blackness. She had stood rock solid just back from the door ready for the attack, But now, her legs began to shake as the initial surge of adrenaline began to ebb. How much longer could she keep this up? She rubbed her eyes. It seemed like the light in the lab was getting brighter. Was the power back on? She shook her head and blinked. Yes, it was much brighter, coming from behind. She spun around and standing in front of her was the strangest man she had ever seen.

HE WAS thin and ragged with wild hair and a thick scrub of beard. The light came from behind him so she could only see him in silhouette. He had come in through the door from the other section of the Medlab, the module they had all assumed to be sealed and derelict. Then came a low buzzing noise and a small robot moved in beside him. It was a little over waist height. It stopped at his side, like a faithful dog.

"Is your colleague still alive?" He pointed over at the unconscious doctor.

"Yes, I think so."

"Gizmo, would you be so kind as to look after the unfortunate individual."

The little robot swung its head around to look up at its master, then it spoke.

"Certainly, Nills." It whizzed over on sleek tracks, extended two arms under the body of the doctor and lifted him up with ease.

"Wait, stop... where are you taking him? Who are you?"

Nills paused and extended his hand. "If you want to stay alive, then you'd better come with us."

12

NILLS & GIZMO

Jann had no real choice. Either stay and face the homicidal Decker, and certain death, or follow the enigmatic colonist and his robotic sidekick to possible safety. So she followed them tentatively through the door and into the wide, brightly lit module. It was empty save for a large section of flooring, hinged up to reveal a long ramp sloping down into the subsurface. The little robot descended first. Nills turned to Jann and waved his hand towards the tunnel. "Quick, follow Gizmo."

As she descended she could hear him closing the floor panel behind them. The light extinguished and the tunnel grew dim, lit solely by illumination from an open airlock door just ahead. Jann had a feeling that she was entering the proverbial rabbit hole.

They passed through the airlock and into a spacious

underground cavern. It was hard to take it all in at once as it was dimly lit, with only patches of illumination here and there. The floor was flat and solid, and looked to be fashioned from some type of concrete. The sections of cave wall that Jann could see shimmered and glistened like they had been coated with some sort of sealant. The area was furnished like a workshop with equipment and machines of indeterminate function. Computer racks and monitors rested on scattered workbenches.

"Gizmo, would you be so kind as to place the injured human over there."

The little robot wheeled around and set Paolio down on a bed with an uncanny gentleness. The doctor was still unconscious. He badly needed surgery on his broken leg and he needed blood, none of which was going to happen. There was not much Jann could do for him. His fate was in the lap of the Gods. She took her helmet off and looked over at the ragged colonist. "You're Nills Langthrop."

"Yes, and you are Dr. Jann Malbec. Science Officer with the International Space Agency Mars expedition."

"Yes, how did you know that?"

Nills didn't answer. Instead, he turned and waved a hand towards the little robot. "This is my friend Gizmo." It rocked its head and spoke.

"Greetings Earthling," said Gizmo.

"Eh... pleased to meet you," she replied, a little uncertain.

She turned back to Nills. "Where are we? Are there any more colonists?"

"All in good time. For the moment you are safe."

"Why were you hiding from us? We've been searching everywhere."

He went quiet and scratched his beard. "It's a long story."

"Nills, I think the infected Earthling is getting ready to leave." Gizmo was over by a bank of monitors. Nills rushed over, followed by Jann. On screen was a video feed from the main Colony One airlock entrance. Decker was putting on his EVA suit. They stood in silence for a while and watched.

"You know what's wrong with him, don't you?" said Jann.

"He's infected. You all probably are." He turned to face Jann who was visibly shocked. "But don't worry, it only affects some. You're okay, as is your colleague," he nodded over at the unconscious Paolio.

"This is what you were talking about... in your last message."

Nills nodded. "So you got that, interesting."

"There must be something we can do."

"Wait, just wait. Come, are you hungry?" He stood up and gestured in the direction of a makeshift galley.

"What? No. It's not exactly high on my list of priorities at the moment. What about Annis, do you know if she's still alive?"

"Patience, we have plenty of time." He walked off, the little robot followed after him. Nills sat down at another row of workstations and started looking at readouts on several monitors. Jann had so many questions going around in her head it was hard to know where to start. But it was clear that Nills was not going to respond well to an intense interrogation. She would have to take it slow. She was not in any immediate danger, as far as she could tell, so there was that at least. Jann also got the impression that Nills had the situation under control, as far as possible. So she decided to take a different tack.

"Yes, I'm really hungry."

His face lit up. "Good, come on, follow me." He jumped up from the workstation and gave a kind of a nod to Gizmo. The little robot reciprocated by rocking its head as they moved over to the galley.

"Gizmo, perhaps you would be so kind as to decant some of that cider we've been saving for a special occasion."

"Excellent idea, Nills. Now would seem like the perfect time. Considering that we have guests with us," the robot replied.

Jann watched it go about its task. It had a kind of scrapyard construction with bits attached here and there. It rode around on tri-pointed tracked wheels and had a speed and grace of movement that spoke of superb engineering skill. She had never seen, or heard of anything like it before.

"Do you like fish?" Nills was staring into a tall storage unit, like a teenager surveying the contents of a fridge.

"Fish would be lovely." She wasn't sure if it would be

lovely. But it seemed to be the best way to engage with the enigmatic Nills.

"Excellent. We have some top notch fish pie left over from our last baking day."

"Good choice, Nills. It should still be well within optimal safety limits for human consumption," the robot interjected.

Nills and Gizmo busied themselves bringing food and plates over to a table. The both moved with a practiced ease, they knew each other's ways. For Jann it was like watching a surreal ballet.

"Come, sit... and tuck in."

There was fish pie, fruit, bread and an assortment of other food of uncertain provenance. As she sat, Gizmo poured her a cup of cider.

"We call it colony cider." Nills raised his cup to her. Jann did likewise and they clinked.

"To new friends," said Nills.

"To new friends." She took a sip and was surprised to find it was absolutely delicious. She downed the whole cup in no time. Gizmo refilled it for her.

"Thank you Gizmo," she said.

"Not at all, my pleasure. It's good that you are enjoying it."

"Yes, it's... delicious." Jann had just entered a whole new world. One where she was having a conversation with a robot, over dinner.

"Your robot is extraordinary."

Nills looked at his creation. "He's my friend."

"Its language skills are remarkable. I'm used to robots saying things like *'stand clear of the doors'* or *'mind the gap.'*"

"Indeed," he nodded. "Tell me, what do you think of the pie?"

Jann was cognizant that, at the same time as she was tucking in, the psychotic Decker was still at large. Kevin and Lu were dead and Paolio was... dying, not to mention the whereabouts of Annis. But, to get anything out of Nills and his robotic friend she would have to work at his pace, on his terms, and that meant trying some pie first. Then a thought crossed her mind. "Maybe he's the cause, maybe he's trying to poison all of us?" Prolonged exposure to isolation can do strange things to the human mind. "Perhaps he's the one who's really mad. Or am I just being paranoid?"

Nills took a forkful of pie and proceeded to eat it, with relish. Comforted by this, Jann placed a tentative morsel in her mouth and ate it. "Mmmmmm... this is absolutely amazing." And it was. After spending months living of ISA prepackaged rations it tasted fantastic.

"Do you hear that Gizmo? She loves it."

"But of course, Nills. I have always said your culinary skills were bordering on the epicurean."

"You flatter me, Gizmo."

"Well, credit where credit is due, as they say. More cider, Doctor Malbec?"

"Eh... sure... okay. Thank you."

"Not at all, it's my pleasure. Please... drink up." It gestured with its free arm at her cup. Jann sat transfixed by the quirky robot. It was more polite and considerate than a lot of dates she'd been on. She began to relax and eat. Hunger got the better of her paranoia. It helped that the food was delicious and she didn't stop until she had cleared her plate. All the while sipping on the colony cider between mouthfuls of fish pie. This seemed to please Nills no end as he kept smiling and nodding at Gizmo, who reciprocated with a kind of Indian head wobble. Then it beeped, and its head turned to look off into the distance, like it was thinking. "What is it?" Nills asked.

"The ISA Commander, Robert Decker, has left the colony," it said.

"Excellent, come, let's get the power back on and get to work." Nills jumped up from the table and scurried over to the workstations. His fingers danced across a keyboard and he muttered to himself as he inspected screen readouts.

"So it was you who switched the power off." Jann had just finished off the last of her cider.

"Yes, yes." He waved a dismissive hand in the air.

"Why did you do that?" Jann ventured.

"The infected. The drop in temperature quiets them down for a while, they become more rational, less volatile." He turned back to his workstation. "How are we doing Gizmo?"

"Rebooting sequentially as planned... all sectors

nominal... optimal temperature in approximately twenty two minutes."

"Good, keep an eye on power distribution."

"Biodome ranging at two point seven"

"Watch acceleration drift."

"Compensating."

"Sub-system deviance?"

"Standard, minus oh point three."

It was evident to Jann that Gizmo was somehow connected into the Colony One systems. Like a sort of remote control unit that monitored and gave feedback to Nills. They also seemed to have established a strange evolved lexicon that only they could understand.

"The commander, where's he going? Where's Annis, is she still alive? Jann was getting more animated.

Nills stood up and surveyed her with a quizzical expression. "I understand you have a lot of questions. We're pretty certain your commander is heading back to your habitation module. We will now lockdown the colony so he can't get back in, at least not easily. We don't know where your first officer is. But once we have power restored, we can do a full sensory analysis of the facility, we'll find her then. Come, we need to look after your injured friend, and Gizmo and myself have many things to tend to in the garden. We can talk later and I will do my best to answer your questions then. In the meantime you're safe."

Jann was taken aback by this uncharacteristic flood of

information. "Okay, thank you. I understand." She walked over to where Paolio was lying. He was regaining consciousness and started moaning and twisting with pain. "We'll need to bring him back up to the medlab so I can do a proper job on that leg."

"Gizmo, can you do the honors?" Nills waved at the injured doctor.

"Certainly," replied the robot as it lifted him up and whizzed off towards the airlock.

13

ANNIS & MALBEC

With power back on in the facility the temperature had risen, it was no longer as cold. Gizmo placed Paolio back on the operating table in the medlab and started a full body scan. A large donut shaped apparatus moved slowly along the length of the table, producing a narrow ribbon of light across his body as it traveled. The resultant image rendered itself on a nearby monitor.

"Fractured collarbone, two fractured ribs," Gizmo zoomed in on Paolio's leg. "You did a good job resetting that fibula."

Nills took his leave. "I need to get to operations and do a complete check on all colony systems. I'll leave you in Gizmo's good hands. He knows where everything is."

For over an hour they worked on Paolio: giving him

morphine, setting up a plasma transfusion, stitching up his leg. The little robot moved with a fast, fluid confidence—Jann was mesmerized. It had the ability to rotate its body three hundred sixty degrees around its tracked base. It had two arms, each with a great number of articulations, giving it the ability to do things no human arm could possibly do. On one, it had a hand of sorts, three fingers and a thumb. On the other, it had the ability to snap on and off different tools which were attached to its body. Its head, if you could call it that, also had the ability to rotate completely and consisted mainly of sensors and antenna. After awhile, she noticed it had no real front or back. Whichever way it pointed its head was front. It would zip over to the operating table, perform some function, rotate its head a hundred and eighty degrees and zip back the way it came.

BY THE TIME they had finished, Paolio's face had regained some of its color, gone was the deathly pallor. The attention they had given the stricken doctor was evidently having a beneficial effect on his physiology. They had pumped him full of morphine, so it would be quite a while before woke up again. But at least he was out of danger. Gizmo surveyed his handiwork. "Your colleague is maintaining a status compatible with life. I would say he has an 86% chance of surviving the next twenty-four hours."

Jann looked at the quirky little robot. It had such a

strange way with words. Symptomatic of its programmer's eccentricities, no doubt.

"Thank you Gizmo—for what you did for him." Jann wasn't quite sure why she kept thanking it. What would its silicon brain understand of gratitude? But it seemed like the right thing to do.

"Don't mention it; it is my pleasure to assist. I would advocate a lengthy rest period of six to eight weeks for the patient. After which he will require some physiotherapy to regain strength in the damaged member."

"Indeed. Tell me Gizmo, how long have you been, eh… aware?"

"Aware of what?

"I mean, when were you switched on?"

"Ahh… yes, you need to ask me a direct question for a direct answer. Otherwise my responses may be as obtuse as the question is vague."

"I see."

"One thousand, one hundred and fifty-eight sols… approximately."

Jann did some quick mental calculations. "Three years. So you were created after the collapse of the colony."

"One thousand, one hundred and fifty-eight sols… approximately," it repeated.

It was built as a friend to keep the castaway sane, his very own Man Friday. "Why did Commander Decker go crazy and start killing our crew?"

"I possess insufficient data to answer that."

"You need to frame a question carefully to get the best response from Gizmo." Nills entered the medlab. He had cleaned himself up and donned a new jumpsuit. Perhaps, before the arrival of the ISA crew, he had no motivation for personal grooming. But now that he had guests, it jumped several notches up his to do list. He looked younger than his thirty-six years and very healthy. A diet of fresh fish and vegetables would probably do that to a person. He turned to face the little robot. "Gizmo, extrapolate probable causes of ISA crew member Commander Decker's psychotic behavior."

"The most likely cause is he succumbed to the very same malaise as the previous members of Colony One"

"Well that doesn't tell us much," said Jann.

"No, but it's the correct answer. He can only work with what he knows already. And I created him after all the mayhem so he has no specific knowledge of it."

"He's an incredible creation nonetheless, with an extraordinary turn of phrase."

"Ha, yes. Sometimes I regret using the complete works of Oscar Wilde as the basis for his grammatical syntax."

"So that's where he gets it. Must have taken you quite a while to build him."

"Well, I did have a lot of time on my hands. He started just as a service bot, for lifting and moving. After a while I integrated him into the colony systems so he could monitor status and alert me to any malfunction. Eventually I programmed him with self learning, neural-net algorithms." He turned and placed an affectionate hand on Gizmo's shoulder. "He's my friend, he's my sanity."

The little robot looked up at its master, like a faithful dog. If it had a tail it would be wagging it right now. Then it twitched and spun its head around, like it was looking off into the distance. Jann had seen it do this once before when Decker left the colony. "Temperature anomaly in fish farm, third quadrant."

"Extrapolate." replied Nills.

"It is consistent with a human life form—it's also moving."

"Annis!" shouted Jann, and she rushed off, with Nills and Gizmo trailing in her wake.

SHE RAN INTO THE BIODOME, past the remains of the door that Decker had broken through. The entrance to the fish farm was strewn with smashed up electronics. She picked up a broken circuit board and showed it to Nills. "The remote comms unit. Annis was using this to send her report back to mission control."

They heard a moan. "Annis?" Jann ventured down the long tunnel and spotted the first officer sitting on the ground with her back to the wall. "Annis... are you okay?"

The first officer looked up and glared. "Malbec?" She

held one hand to her head in and Jann could see it was covered in blood.

"Decker's gone crazy... attacked me with a steel bar... totally berserk." She looked up and her eyes widened with fright. She shifted and started to back away. "Malbec, there's someone out there!" She pointed towards the entrance.

"It's all right, Annis. This is Nills Langthorp, a colonist."

Nills waved.

"Is that... a robot?"

"Yes, that's Gizmo."

Gizmo raised his hand to wave. "Greetings, Earthling."

Annis stared at the pair for a moment. "So he's the ghost we've been hunting."

"Yes, he was hiding out."

"And where's that crazy bastard Decker?"

"Gone. Left the Colony a few hours ago. Went back to the HAB."

"The others?"

Jann hesitated. "Paolio is pretty banged up. Kevin and Lu are... dead."

"Oh shit." Annis slumped down and held her head. "What a mess."

"Come, let's get you to the medlab." Jann helped her up.

As they moved out into the biodome Nills approached them. "We have work to do in the garden here. I'll check in on you later."

"Sure, thanks."

. . .

THE FIRST OFFICER sat on a seat in the medlab as Jann tended to the wound on her head. She brought her up to speed on all that had happened. Like Jann, Annis got lucky. Decker attacked her in the biodome while she was sending her report. She retaliated by throwing the comms unit at Decker. This seemed to distract him and the unit now became the threat in Decker's deranged mind. He proceeded to smash it into tiny pieces, giving Annis time to hide out under a tank in the fish farm—where she eventually passed out from the blow to her head.

"We should really do an x-ray to see if there's a fracture," said Jann.

Annis brushed her aside. "I'm fine." She stood up. "No time for that now. We need to deal with that crazy Decker or he'll destroy this mission."

Before Jann had time to answer Nills and Gizmo entered the medlab. "How are you feeling?"

Annis stared at them for a moment, looking from one to the other. "I'm fine. You got any ideas what the commander is up to now?"

"Gizmo, extrapolate possible current scenario for ISA crewmember Robert Decker," said Nills.

"Based on the historical data sets available, subjects tend to engage in a repeated pattern of deep sleep, followed by psychosis, then by a short period of rationality. Your commander has a 72.6% probability of being asleep at this time. But this is based on the limited data at my disposal."

Annis was visibly in awe at the response from the little robot. It took her a moment to adjust to this new reality.

"Well, if that's true, then it doesn't give us much time," she said.

"Why? What are you going to do?" said Jann.

"You mean what are *we* going to do. Well, it's simple. We're going to kill him."

"What? No, you're joking, you can't do that."

"That would indeed increase your mission success probability by a factor of 82.6%. Allowing for other unforeseen events," offered Gizmo.

"No way, I won't do it."

"Listen, Lu and Kevin are dead, Paolio's in bad shape and I'm getting seriously pissed off. So you better start growing a set of balls, Malbec. We're going to do this—we have to do it —and, if that robot thing is right, we're running out of time."

Jann thought about it and Annis had a point. If what Nills told her about the progress of the condition was correct, then the commander would only get worse. What alternatives did they have? The only other option was to somehow contain him safely, for both the rest of the mission here and on the long journey back. Cooped up on the Odyssey transit craft for two and a half months with a psychotic Decker was not a prospect that anyone would relish. But to kill him—that seemed brutally cold to Jann. "There has to be a better way."

"Like what? Appeal to his feminine side?" snapped Annis.

"Your first officer is right," interjected Nills, who was in the process of opening drawers and lockers looking for something. "His condition will only deteriorate. He'll drift in and out of psychosis until eventually he will be completely insane." He was reading the labels on various packages he had liberated from one of the medlab lockers. He looked over at Jann and Annis. "There is no hope for him now. You must realize he is beyond redemption."

"I can't accept that. There must be something we can do for him," said Jann.

"Like what, find a cure?" said Annis.

"Nills, you must know something about what causes this."

"I've told you all I know. It only affects some people, male and female equally. They go mad with rage, become crazed psychotic killers. I don't know how or why." He scratched his chin as if he had thought of something. "If I were to hazard a guess I'd say it's a bacterial infection."

"What makes you think that?" said Jann.

"I don't know... it's just a... feeling."

"Enough of this. We're wasting time. Do you have anything we can use as weapons?" said Annis.

Nills tossed a small plastic package over to her. "Here. It's cyclophromazine. There are three doses in there, each in separate syringes. That should be enough to kill him."

"Wait a minute. If it's bacterial then have you tried just using a dose of antibiotics?"

Nills paused before answering, "Well, no. We were too busy trying to stay alive. It's hard to play doctors and patients when the patient is trying to bash your head in."

"So it might work?" Jann looked at them both in turn.

"Attention... Commander Decker is on the move," squeaked Gizmo.

"Quick. Follow me... this way." Nills raced out of the medlab and into the main Colony One operations area. He flicked a display table to life and a 3D rendering of the northwestern area of the Jezero crater ballooned out from its surface. They could see the colony on one side. Farther out were the HAB and lander. A red marker flashed beside the HAB. Nills pointed at it. "That's Decker. Gizmo's right, he's left your HAB module."

"Of course I'm right."

Annis turned to the quirky robot. "I thought you said that he would sleep for hours."

"Gizmo did, but it came with a 72.6% probability caveat. So this action is in the other 27.4%."

They all watched the blip as it moved away from the HAB and then stopped. "What's he doing?" said Jann.

"He probably doesn't know himself," said Nills.

"We're wasting time. We need to get out there and take him in the open." Annis was heading over to get her helmet. Jann was now looking at the package containing the cyclophromazine. "There's no way this is going to penetrate an EVA suit. The needle is too short."

"Shit," said Annis. By now the blip was on the move again. "Looks like he's heading this way." Nills pointed to the marker on the map.

Jann considered what to do. They should at least try and contain the commander. That way they could help him and maybe even shed some light on the source of the affliction. "I think we should attempt comms, try and assess his state of mind."

"Are you joking? That might be just a red flag to a bull."

"Dr. Malbec has a point," said Nills. "If he's semi-rational then you might be able to contain him more easily. If he's not, then it's not going to make any difference."

Before Annis could answer Jann had strapped on her suit headset and pressed broad transmit. "Commander Decker, this is Dr. Malbec, what's your status, over."

There was silence. Jann tried again. "Commander Decker, this is..."

"I hear you. Where is everybody? What's going on?"

They all exchanged looks, like partners in crime, a conspiracy unfolding. Annis grabbed her headset, put it on and listened in. "We're in the colony. How are you feeling?"

"They're crawling all over me... I can't get rid of them... gnawing at my brain... I need to scratch them out... this... this contamination."

"Just stay calm, we'll help you."

More silence. "Commander?" Then there was a sickening cry from the comms. Jann and Annis exchanged looks. Nills wore a concerned face, tinged with an experienced acceptance—he'd seen it all before.

"Decker, can you hear me?" Silence. Jann whipped the headset off and flung it down. "We'd better get ready."

"What's he sound like?" said Nills. "Batshit crazy, going on about 'contamination.' It makes no sense."

Jann looked at the blip on the 3D map. It was moving steadily towards them.

"Can we trap him in the airlock?" Annis directed her question at Nills.

"And then what? Wait till his air runs out?"

"Is that possible?"

"No, wait, let's think. If we can contain him and get him sedated, then maybe we could find out what's causing this," said Jann.

"Jesus, Jann. If we let him in here he'll kill us or we'll get seriously injured before we can take him out. No way."

"We just need him to take his helmet off before he leaves the airlock. Then we jab him in the neck, he'll go down in a few seconds."

"Gizmo thinks the probability of successfully containing your Commander Decker without sustaining injury is 0.1%," said the little robot.

"Thanks for the analysis," replied Jann.

"Don't mention it, my pleasure. I'm here to help," said Gizmo.

"We're going to need some weapons. What have you got, Nills?" said Annis.

"Knives, heavy tools, steel bars."

"Okay, show me." They moved over to the workshop and in a few minutes Annis returned holding a long sharp knife in one hand and a heavy tool in the other. "Here's the deal. If he doesn't take his helmet off he stays in the airlock. If he does, and you don't get that syringe into to him, then the first step he takes I'm going to gut him, no hesitation. Got that?"

Jann nodded. The red blip was almost at the door.

IOCC OF CYCLOPHROMAZINE would be more than enough to drop a large man in seconds. 20cc and it would be fifty-fifty if he lived. 30cc and he's dead—no question. It was 5cc that Dr. Corelli jabbed into her when she lost it in the colony. Things had changed since then. Two crew were dead and the tables had turned. She broke the seal on the package and fumbled with the hypodermic. It seemed a very insubstantial weapon in the face of such a raging bull as the demented Decker. "Hold fast old girl—focus," she said to herself.

"At the door!" Annis had taken up position right at the interior airlock door. She had the look of a warrior, the long knife held at the ready. Jann looked around to find that Nills and Gizmo had disappeared. "Where's Nills?"

"Screw him, we don't need him. This is our shit to sort out. Are you ready to do this, Jann? Because if you're not then we keep him in the airlock and watch him die."

Jann hurried over to the door and steeled herself. "Okay, ready." They heard the *whirr* of the pump as it started to depressurize. The alert indicator flashed red as the exterior door opened and in stepped Commander Decker. It was a tentative step at first. Like a wild animal sniffing out a strange box in the forest. Driven on by scent, held back by fear, uncertain of its surroundings. The door automatically closed behind him as he spotted Jann and Annis through the interior door observation window. He raced forward and crashed into it. They jumped back. Jann was shaken by the ferocity of the attack. He banged at the door several more times and then paused.

"Jesus, he's pretty pissed. I say we just go with plan A and keep him locked in there until he runs out of air."

"Do you know how to switch off the air?"

They both realized that they didn't know. The only one who did was Nills and he had gone back into hiding. "Shit, no."

"What's he doing?"

Annis peered through the little window again. "Just standing there. Wait a minute, I think he's taking his helmet off." Jann came back to the window and joined her. His face was blotchy red and scratched. Blood had congealed along his forehead and matted his hair. He looked at them but didn't move. He seemed to be in pain and his face contorted as he brought his hands up to cradle his head. He mouthed a scream and dropped to his knees, he shook his head like he was trying to get something out that was gnawing away at his brain.

Jann looked on in horror at this forlorn figure. A pale and tormented shadow of the Decker that commanded the ISA Mars mission. There was no rethinking this. She needed to help him if she could. Somewhere inside that tortured creature was still the soul of a human, one that needed to be saved, not killed. She looked over at Annis. The first officer was ready to kill him to save the mission. It was simply a matter of calculating the odds with her. The mission came first. The human second.

Jann readied herself. Time to do this. "Okay, let's open the door now he's down. I'll stick him in the neck with this and that should take him down."

"You really want to do this?"

Jann nodded and placed a hand on the door release. She held the hypodermic high, ready to stab down at the first opportunity. Annis stood to her left, ready to end his life if need be.

Jann hit the door release and slowly began to ease it open. Then something must have clicked in Decker's tormented brain because he lunged at the door with tremendous speed. Jann was sent tumbling backwards across the floor with the force of impact. The syringe fell from her hand and skidded under a mound of workshop parts. "Damn."

She tasted blood in her mouth, her face hurt like hell and her right eye was closing up. "Shit." Annis failed to counter Decker's attack and he grabbed her knife hand at the wrist, the other hand on her throat, pinning her down to a workshop table. She kicked and fought but it had no effect. Decker was simply too strong and too crazed. "Shit, where's the syringe?" Jann got on all fours and tried to find it. She had better hurry or Annis would be dead. She spotted it, picked it up and bounded over to Decker. He saw her coming, turned and literally threw Annis at her. In one-third gravity she sailed through the air like a rag doll. Jann ducked as Annis crashed down across a pile of machine parts. Decker grinned. Jann stood her ground. They faced off.

He lunged. But it was primal, there was no fighting skill there. Simply the wild flailing of a rabid animal. Jann, on the other hand had a skill, kickboxing. It was a hobby, a way of keeping fit, nothing more—until now. She saw the way he moved, his momentum. She twisted sideways and brought the needle down on his neck—except she missed, the needle hitting the metal neck rim of his EVA suit. Decker careened past her and crashed to the ground. He slid along it with the force of his own momentum. The needle was broken.

"Shit." Jann rummaged in the pockets of her flight suit to extract another one. But Decker was already on the attack. Again she dodged but this time she swung a kick and caught him across the side of the head. He felt it because he crashed face down on the floor and took a moment to recover. Annis was now back on her feet and looking for the knife. Before Decker had time to get to his feet, Jann swung another kick to the head and again he went down. Annis found the knife and was ready to dispatch him when Jann finally jumped on Decker and jabbed him in the neck with the hypodermic. He looked at her with a kind of shocked surprise, then his eyes closed and he slumped to the floor.

Jann rolled off him, breathing heavily and shaking with adrenaline. Her face hurt like hell. Annis came over and offered her a hand. Jann grabbed it and pulled herself up. "Where did you learn to kick like that?"

Jann shrugged. "I work out."

"You're one real badass—respect." She patted Jann on the shoulder.

They looked down at the forlorn Decker. "That bastard nearly killed me." Annis kicked him hard in the gut a few times. Decker didn't move. "Is he dead?"

"No, but he's out for the count for a few hours. Come on let's get him tied up before he comes around. Drag him into the medlab."

PAOLIO, still unconscious, occupied the only bed in the medlab. But his injuries paled in comparison to the torment that afflicted Decker, so Jann had no qualms about relocating him to the floor, while Decker took up residence in his stead. Fortunately, the medlab operating table had restraints built in. Why, Jann didn't know, nor did she care. They laid him out, strapped him down, and double checked. Then Nills showed up.

"Well, where the hell were you? Hiding in your hole, no doubt." Annis was pissed.

"It's served me well in the past. In case you haven't noticed. I'm the only one left alive in here. I see you have managed to incapacitate the afflicted crewmember."

"No thanks to you," replied Annis.

"Enough," said Jann. Her face hurt when she talked. She was exhausted—mentally, physically and emotionally. She sat down, grabbed a mirror and brought it up to her face. It wasn't too bad. Not as bad as it felt. Just a lot of bruising. Could be worse, much worse. She could be dead.

Annis sat across from her rubbing her neck. "You know, I need to get a report back to mission control. They'll be wondering what the hell is going on up here."

"We have no comms unit, remember? Decker smashed it to pieces."

"I'll do it from the HAB."

"Can't it wait?"

"No, it's got to be done. I'll take the mule, let it drive me." She stood up and stretched her shoulders. "Let's hope Decker hasn't trashed the HAB."

14

CAVES

Jann set up an IV drip to keep Decker sedated—to keep his violence in check. He was comatose and she hoped he would stay that way until she got a handle on the cause of his psychosis. And if she didn't, then what? Let him die?

"Come, I'll show you where you can sleep." Nills beckoned to Jann from the medlab entrance. Gizmo gently lifted Paolio off the floor. They weren't going to leave him here, not on the floor and certainly not with Decker. The doctor was beginning to come around, he moaned and cried out as Gizmo carried him. Jann held his hand. "It's all right Paolio, we'll get you comfortable." They all moved off to an accommodation module and the medlab was locked down— just in case.

There were several of these modules dotted all over

Colony One. Nills had powered up a unit just off the main common area. It was designed for twelve. They put Paolio in one of the bunks and settled him in.

"There's a shower in here, if you want to freshen up."

Jann slumped down on a bunk opposite Paolio. "Thanks Nills."

"Okay, we'll leave you alone now. If you need anything, I'll be in the biodome." He left, Gizmo trailing after him.

"MALBEC?" Jann pressed the headset closer to her ear; the signal from Annis was distorted. The Colony One radiation shielding was playing havoc with the comms.

"Annis, yes, I'm here."

"The HAB is trashed. That crazy bastard wrecked the place."

"How bad is it?"

"He must have gone berserk inside, smashing things up. It's still got integrity, life support is okay. Mostly it's just the equipment inside, things strewn everywhere. The coffee machine is history."

"Paolio's not going to be happy to hear that."

"Well that's the least of our problems. The comms unit is dead."

"What?"

"We have no way to contact mission control."

"Can it be fixed?"

"*I don't know. I'm going to run some tests and do an audit on the damage. I'll touch base with you in the morning.*"

"Are you staying in the HAB tonight?"

"*Damn right. I'm not spending any more time in that colony than I have to. If you want to stay over there and play mommy, that's your problem. I'll see you in the morning—assuming you're still alive.*"

The comms disconnected. *Jesus,* thought Jann. *A whole new level of obnoxiousness—great.*

HER SLEEP WAS fitful as her mind spent most of the night contemplating the malaise that had turned Decker into a homicidal maniac. She rationalized the obvious first. It manifested itself as an altered mental state, probably due to a chemical imbalance within the brain. This could be caused by drugs, but she thought that unlikely. The other possibility was an infection, viral or bacterial. Either one could theoretically cause an imbalance. Nills had intimated that it was bacterial. But this was not based on any scientific analysis. It was simply an assumption on his part. Of course, Jann couldn't rule out the possibility that it might be of alien origin.

"DR. MALBEC, WAKE UP." Nills shook her gently. "Dr. Malbec..."

"Eh... what..." Jann opened her eyes and stared up at the strange figure. As her sleep-fogged mind cleared, she remembered where she was. "I fell asleep. How long was I out?"

"Eight hours. I was going to wake you earlier but you looked so peaceful so I left you."

She sat up rigid. "Decker?"

"Still there... still comatose."

She sighed, relaxed a bit and then realized Paolio was also awake. He was alert and sitting up in the bunk talking to Gizmo—in Italian.

"Paolio!"

"Jann, you're still alive I see," he smiled. He was in good spirits, gone was the deathly pallor of the previous day. He was anxious to learn all that had happened, so they talked for a time. Nills and Gizmo left them to it, but returned a short while later with a homemade, motorized wheelchair.

"Here. This might be useful. We made it... eh... for Marcella, I think. Long time ago now. She injured her ankle doing some stupid low-gravity stunt... can't remember what it was exactly. Anyway, I checked it out and it still works pretty well."

Jann lifted Paolio out of the bunk and helped him into the wheelchair. She found the low-gravity tremendously empowering. To lift such seemingly heavy weights just didn't get old for her. Paolio's broken leg was kept extended by virtue of a metal truss attached to the seat. He played with the controls to gain some familiarity with their function.

"I should go check on Decker," said Jann.

"I'm coming with you."

"You should really be resting, Paolio. Not taxing your body any more than necessary."

He looked up at her and smiled. "Who's the doctor here? Anyway, I think I've got the hang of this thing, let's go. Lead the way." He tapped the joystick and followed Jann to the medlab.

The commander was still strapped on the operating table where they had left him the previous night. His life drawn out on the monitors in green and blue phosphorescent waves. Paolio spent some time examining him and checking his vitals. "Well, he's not going anywhere for a while," he said when he had finished. "How do you think we should proceed?"

"Let's start with blood, that might give us some clues." Jann looked around the medlab. "This place is reasonably well equipped. It's got everything we need to make a start. And then there's that research lab, on the other side of the facility. That may prove useful if it can be brought back online. I wonder what they were doing in there?"

Paolio shrugged his good shoulder and smiled. "Research?"

"Greetings." Gizmo whizzed in. "Nills has requested you

join us in the common room for some breakfast—at your convenience, of course."

Jann looked down at Paolio. "Hungry?"

"Starving."

"Come on then, Decker's safe enough here for now. Let's get some food."

NILLS AND GIZMO had been busy. They had set out an array of food on the main table in the common area. Standard colony fare: fresh fruit, salads and fish. There was also a good supply of colony cider. Nills sat in a battered chair eating a bowl of porridge.

"Just so you know," said Nills between mouthfuls of food, "The bodies of your deceased colleagues have been stored in an exterior unit, where it's subzero."

Jann sat down and put her head in her hands. Paolio leaned over and patted her back. She grabbed his hand with both of hers, pressed it against her cheek and sobbed. It had finally sunk in, the tragedy of it. She couldn't control it, and it all came flooding over her and her body shook.

"Dr. Malbec?" Gizmo's voice was surprisingly low, as if the little robot could somehow sense the emotion of the moment. Jann lifted her head, released Paolio's hand and rubbed a moist eye. "Yes?"

"Would you like some tea?"

She managed a smile and nodded. "Sure, thanks."

"Make that two," said Paolio, he too was visibly emotional. The death of Lu was particularly hard for him. He patted Jann's back one last time as the moment passed and they both regained some composure.

"Tell us what happened here, Nills. You've seen all this before, haven't you?"

Nills put down the now empty bowl and scratched his chin. "I have, it seems a long time ago now. It's what destroyed the colony—well almost."

"So what the hell is it? We need to know. Two of us are dead and our commander is a raging psycho. What do we do?" Jann's frustration was bubbling to the surface.

"There's nothing you can do, except run and hide."

Gizmo arrived with mugs of tea and Jann took a tentative sip. It was surprisingly good. She relaxed, got some control of her emotions. She needed to get the story out of Nills, but it was evident he would do it in his own time. There was nothing to be gained by pushing him. Nills sipped his tea, took a rolled up cigarette out of his pocket and lit it. He blew the smoke out in a long satisfying plume. He offered it to the others. "Fancy a toke?"

Paolio reached over and took the joint. Jann looked over at him. He waved a hand and shrugged his good shoulder again. "Hey, pain, you know."

Nills opened up. "It started after the second phase of the colony was built, after the research lab. We don't know why it happened or what caused it. But some of us just started going off the rails. In the beginning it was like... just one or two people. The symptoms were a type of psychosis that affected just the individual. I mean, they had no desire to kill anybody. The first colonist to die was Peter Jensen. He suffered very badly from this illness. And then, one day, he just walked into the airlock without an EVA suit and depressurized it. It took us days to clean him off the walls."

"Days, really?" said Jann.

"Well, no. That's a bit of an exaggeration, but let's just say it wasn't pretty."

Paolio coughed and passed the joint back. Nills took another drag, blew out the smoke and continued. "COM knew all this, of course, but they were at a loss as to what was causing the colonists to go stark raving mad. Eventually it got so bad that a few of them decided to decamp to the mining outpost."

"The one over at the far side of the crater?" said Jann

"Yeah."

"But I thought that had only minimal life support?"

Nills scratched his chin again and looked from one to the other like he was considering something. "I don't suppose it matters now, so I might as well tell you." Nills waved a hand in a vague direction. "The mining outpost is around ten kilometers north east of here. At the base of a cliff over by the crater rim. It's a vast, mineral rich cave system. It had a relatively small entrance so over time it was sealed with an airlock and pressurized. Once that happened, people began to stay there, and eventually we moved a lot of equipment and many of the modules over there. It was quite impressive. We also had this crazy idea that if anything happened to this place we could survive there."

"How come we didn't know about this?" said Jann. Paolio was coughing again as he passed the last of the joint back to Nills.

"We kept it secret." Nills inspected the butt. "You have to understand, that back then, living here was like living in a fish bowl. Every single microscopic detail of our lives was broadcast to a million different digital media channels back on Earth—twenty-four seven. No one had a private life. So, we just kept it quiet. No cameras, no intrusion, it was our private space."

"Are there still people there, maybe someone still alive?" said Jann.

"No, definitely not. They're all dead."

"How do you know for sure?"

"Look, I just do, okay? The outpost ran using solar panels so they would have run out of power during the storm. If there was someone still alive they would contact me here. No... they're all dead. There's just me and Gizmo left now." He took a last drag of the joint and stubbed the butt out on a metal plate. Then he just sort of zoned out. Jann wasn't sure if he was thinking or had simply stopped talking.

"So what happened during the sandstorm?" she prompted.

"Oh, eh... yes, the sandstorm. Well that was a total mess if ever there was one. It wasn't a big deal at the start, we were used to them. But after the first month we had the bright idea to start conserving power. That's when people really started to go nuts—like your commander. People were dying as we fought to get the crazies under control. But as soon as one was dealt with another would go nuts, then another and another. It was mayhem. We managed to get some contained in the far dome, that's when the plutonium power source failed." He clicked his fingers. "Just like that, bang, gone. Now we were in real trouble. If we didn't get it back online then all we had for power was the solar array and that was worse than useless during the storm."

"So what did you do?"

"We assumed it had been damaged or sabotaged by the crazies. Some of us ventured outside to try and trace the cables back out to the source—find where the problem was. But they never returned. Some got lost, some were killed... I don't know. Meanwhile, the power was getting critical and more of us were succumbing to the illness. It was scary as you didn't know who would be next. They destroyed the far dome, one of the tunnels and a whole bunch of other stuff."

"How did you survive?"

"Back in the beginning of the colony, we used to process soil on the surface but we accidentally discovered caves," he laughed, "right under us. It was just luck. Anyway, we sealed them up and started using them for soil processing. Much easier than outside on the surface. So, when everything went to rat shit it was a good place to hide." He stopped and seemed to be thinking again.

"So you holed up down there, for how long?" Paolio had now progressed on to a mug of colony cider.

Nills had zoned out again. "Eh… where was I, oh yes, the cave. Three months we spent there. They couldn't find us, too dumb. We would sneak up when they were asleep, when they had stopped trying to kill each other and wrecking the place. We'd grab stuff and bring it back down. Eventually, they all killed each other up top, there was only one left. So we blew him out the airlock."

"And then what?" said Paolio.

"By now we were living off fumes. Very little power left and the facility was ripped apart. Life support was barely functioning. The storm still raged outside."

"So… The windmills in the airlocks…" said Jann.

Nills laughed. "Yeah, that was my bright idea. It helped a bit. But what saved us in the end was a power control system reboot." He started laughing and shaking his head. "It was just so dumb. I was trying to conserve as much power as possible by hacking the software on the mainframe, switching things off that it regarded as essential. I took the risk of doing a cold reboot—and what do you know?" Nills was on the edge of his seat now, waving his hands. "The goddamn plutonium power source came back online." He started laughing hysterically. "We were just a bunch of dumb idiots, we never thought to try it before, kept thinking it was the crazies that were causing it." He collapsed back in his seat. "And that was that. We survived."

"We?" said Jann

Nills went quiet for a time, eventually he spoke again. "I don't want to talk about that... not now, some other time... maybe."

"Why didn't you contact Earth and let them know?"

"The storm destroyed the uplink antenna."

"But you could have written an S.O.S on the sand or something."

"And then what? What would happen?"

"Well Earth would send people and supplies."

"Yes. That's exactly what they would do. And look how that turned out." He looked across at Jann and Paolio. "Not so good, don't you think? Two of your crew are dead." He sat back. "No, there was no way we wanted any more people up here. Not until we found out what was causing this psychosis."

"So did you discover anything?"

"Not much. I suspect it's some type of bacterial infection. It started a while after the research lab was built. New people came, geneticists. The rumor was COM was even going to return them to Earth. That didn't go down well with the rest of us." He waved a dismissive hand in the air. "I don't know, maybe it was just crazy talk."

"So what were they doing, these *geneticists*?" Jann kept prompting Nills, now that he was in talkative mood.

"Playing God, screwing with organisms, making money for the Colony One Mars consortium. Although, to be fair, without GM this place wouldn't function."

Jann stood up and started to pace. "There must be more to it than a rogue bacterium, how come only the commander was affected?"

"It only affects some people, and there's no pattern that we could see. Nills downed the last of his tea.

"So, I've told you my story, what about you? You're not COM people."

Jann took up the question. "No, this is an International Space Agency mission. We're here to investigate what happened, gather up a few rocks while we're at it and return to Earth. It's a three month mission."

"Return to Earth?"

"Yes."

"Where is COM in all of this? After all, this is technically their facility."

"Not anymore. They handed it over to ISA."

"That sounds uncharacteristically generous of them. Forgive me if I don't believe it."

"Well, nobody was going to come back here on a one-way ticket and COM didn't have the resources to start all over again. So it made sense to do it this way."

"Let me see if I have this straight. The COM consortium

hands over all their assets up here to the ISA, which don't amount to a hill of beans since they all thought it was derelict. And then, gets national space agencies to spend taxpayer money to get them back up here."

"This is not a COM mission," insisted Jann.

Nills laughed. "Want to know what I think? I think you've all been taken for a ride." He stood up. "Look, do what you need to do. I really don't give a shit anyway." With that, Gizmo seemed to wake up.

"Earthling approaching airlock."

A FEW MOMENTS LATER, First Officer Annis Romanov strode into the common room and straight over to Nills. "Our comms unit is dead in the HAB. We need you to fix it for us."

Nills looked at her with eyes like laser beams. Yet it was Gizmo that spoke. "Nills does not go outside on the planet's surface."

Annis was not sure what to make of this response. She looked at the robot and then back at Nills. "Hey, this is a serious issue. We have no way to contact our mission control.

"Nills does not go out onto the planet's surface," repeated Gizmo.

Before Annis could react Jann interjected. "What if we brought it here, could you look at it for us?"

Nills nodded. "I could do that. No guarantees, though."

"Forget it. I'll fix it myself, said Annis.

"Can you do that?" said Paolio.

"I think so. It will be quicker than taking it apart and bringing it here."

"Problem solved, then," said Nills. "Now if you all don't mind I have a garden that needs attending to." With that, he and Gizmo headed off to the biodome.

Annis slumped down in a chair. "You're all still alive, I see."

"Sleep well, did we?" said Jann.

Annis scowled. "In case you haven't noticed, Kevin and Lu are dead and Decker is a vegetable. As first officer that puts me in command of this mission now, and we need to keep it on track."

"Eat some breakfast and chill out."

She looked at the food with disgust. "How do you know he's not trying to poison us?" I don't trust him—or that goofy robot."

"Actually, when I get back to Earth, I really want one of those things," said Paolio.

"That's assuming we get back," said Jann.

"Look, we've had a major setback, but there's no reason we can't salvage what we can from the mission. The colony still functions and a survivor has been found. This is major and we need to get this information back to COM."

"You mean ISA," Jann was pouring herself some colony cider.

"Yes, yes, I mean ISA." Annis paused for a minute, like

she was considering something and looked from one to the other. "Just so we're all up front," she finally said, "if either of you start going off the rails... I won't hesitate to kill you."

"That's nice of you, Annis. You're such a sweetie," replied Jann.

15

BLOODS

Paolio felt extremely fatigued after the morning's breakfast with Nills. No doubt, the two mugs of colony cider and the smoke had a lot to do with it. Nevertheless, he was still physically fragile after what Decker did to him, so he went back to the accommodation module to rest. Jann headed into the medlab to check on the commander. As for Annis... well Jann wasn't really sure where she went.

There was no change in Decker. His breathing, heart rate and temperature were all still elevated. His skin was a heightened pink color and his body was drenched in sweat, like he was running a high fever. Earlier, Paolio had cleaned up the wound around his forehead. Jann leaned over to inspect the Italian doctor's handiwork. The scratches that Decker had accumulated all over his face were healing fast.

In fact, they were nearly gone. Perhaps the injuries weren't as bad as she had originally thought. Lifting up the bandage covering Decker's head wound, Jann was startled to find that it had also begun to heal. Better mention it to Paolio when he arrived. No doubt he would have an explanation for this seemingly remarkable healing power.

She let him be and turned her attention to the equipment in the medlab. Before embarking on any tests she first needed to do an audit of what was available to her. As a medical surgery it was well equipped and stocked. But for in-depth analysis, she would need something more sophisticated. Possibly the research lab on the other side of the facility had what she needed. But that was offline for the moment. Maybe Nills could be persuaded to get it back up and running. In the meantime, she had a reasonably good microscope at her disposal here, so she could start doing some preliminary investigations.

By late morning she had taken a blood sample from Decker, as well as a number of other swabs, and was now incubating a series of test cultures. If there were any invasive bacteria roaming around in the commander then these tests would go a long way to finding it. However, they needed hours, possibly days, in the incubator before any conclusive results could be ascertained, so she had time to kill. Rather than waste it she made up several slides with a drop of Decker's blood using different stains. She placed the first one under the scope and peered through the lens. She delicately moved and shifted the focus point around the sample, not really expecting to find anything out of the ordinary.

It contained the usual mix of healthy blood biology. She would try and get an approximation of cell count, giving her a base to chart any rise or fall over time. Then something caught her eye. A darkened area; she focused in. A cluster of elongated cells came into view. Jann marked the spot and continued with her visual scan. She found another, and another. She wouldn't need the incubated cultures after all. Decker's blood was teeming with bacteria.

Her first thought was it might be tetanus, a fairly typical blood infection, usually picked up from soil. But it didn't have the right features for her to be certain, and this being Mars, it wasn't in the soil up here. Yet, there was something very familiar about these cells, the elongated rod shape, the waxy surface... she had seen this before. Then it hit her. "Impossible... it can't be."

She sat back and contemplated this discovery. Was this the cause of Decker's psychosis? She stood up and was about to go find Paolio, to give him the news, when another thought entered her head. Maybe she should check her own blood. She wrapped a tourniquet around her upper arm and bit down on the loose end to pull it tight. She clenched her fist, felt her forearm for a suitable vein and identified a candidate. She flicked the cap of a syringe with her thumb and jabbed it in. Jann retracted the plunger and drew up her own blood. Once the plunger could go no further she gently extracted the needle and released the tourniquet. She prepared a slide with a drop from the syringe and placed it under the microscope. After a few moments of searching she sat back in the chair and breathed a sigh of relief... she found nothing. But that didn't mean she wasn't infected. It might still be there in much lower levels. Too few for her to detect with such a tiny random sample. She considered making up another slide, but it would be better to incubate a culture. If there were any bacteria it would grow and multiply in the petri dish. But it would take a long time for a clear result— assuming this was what she thought it was.

Jann heard the whirr of a motor and turned to see Paolio drive in to the medlab in his scrapyard wheelchair. "How's our patient?" he said.

"No change. But have a look at this." She directed him to the microscope and hit a button to bring up a snapshot of Decker's sample on the monitor.

"What am I looking at here?"

"A blood sample from Decker."

Paolio examined the image. "Looks like a pretty bad bacterial infection, any idea what type?"

"I've seen something like this before. But not in blood, only in skin tissue."

Jann looked at Paolio for a moment like she was considering what she was going to say next. "Paolio, how familiar are you with *Mycobacterium Leprae*?"

He thought about this. "*Leprae?*" He tapped his chin with

a finger as he thought. Then it dawned on him. "Leprosy! Are you saying this is leprosy?"

"Do you know anything about the disease?"

Paolio screwed up his face as he delved into the recesses of his memory, trying to resurrect any snippet of information he had stored away. "Let me think. Not something that a medical practitioner comes across these days. I know it's bacterial, affects the nervous system and that around 95% of humans have immunity to it. Other than that, not a lot."

"You're correct, it's bacterial, and it attacks nerve cells. But it can perform a very remarkable trick. What it does is turn nerve cells into stem cells, cells that can become anything: muscle, bone, organs... anything. Not only that, it also alters the human DNA within the cell, a bit like a retrovirus."

"No, I didn't know that."

"As you can imagine, this is of great interest to geneticists. Here's a bacteria that can manufacture stem cells and alter DNA at the same time."

Are you sure that's what it is?"

"I did a thesis on it, that's how I recognized it."

"So, this is leprosy?"

"Well... no. It's something very like it. A lot more virulent for one."

"A mutation?"

"More likely it's been engineered. Probably right here."

"Holy shit." Paolio looked over at the unconscious commander.

"Why? For what purpose? He was looking at the image on the monitor more intently now.

"If you wanted a way to re-engineer a human from the inside. 'Mycobacterium Leprae' gives you the tools. A bacteria that creates stem cells with your very own DNA payload."

Paolio stared wide-eyed at Jann. "Jesus."

"Yes, exactly. Playing God."

Paolio looked back at the image and pointed to the cluster of cells. "Do you think that is the cause of the commander's psychosis?"

"Well, it would seem to be a likely candidate. Then again, it could be something else entirely. If we could get the research lab up and running then I'd be able to do more in-depth analysis. I might be able to sequence it, or at least part of it.

"That could take a while."

They both looked back at the image on the monitor and said nothing for a time.

"What about trying some antibiotics, see if that kills it? It's old-school, but it's just bacteria after all."

"Worth a shot."

"Okay, I'll check what they have here and what we brought with us and see if one of them can kill it. If it does then we might just be able to bring him back."

"I've also checked my own blood."

"And..."

"I found nothing. Nevertheless, I'm doing a culture test, just in case. I'll need to check everyone, though."

Paolio rolled up his sleeve. "I'm sure mine is 80% caffeine."

"Sorry, I feel guilty about taking a blood sample from you. You lost quite a bit already." Jann unpacked a new syringe.

"A few ccs more isn't going to make any difference now."

When Jann had finished Paolio grabbed two more syringes and stuffed them into a pocket. "I'll go and get samples from the others."

"Okay. Oh... before you go, can you have a look at this?"

She walked over to where Decker was lying and lifted the dressing from his head wound. Paolio leaned in and examined him. He looked up at Jann with a raised eyebrow. "That's almost healed. Quite extraordinary."

"That's what I thought, and see here, all the scratches on his face are gone, too." Paolio sat back in his wheelchair and rubbed his chin. "I've never seen anything like it. It's like his body is in overdrive."

"What could cause that?"

"I really don't know." Paolio was about to replace the dressing but there was really no point now. He backed up his chair and sighed. "Things are getting weirder around here." He rolled across the medlab heading for the door. "No point in concerning ourselves with it now. I'll go get samples from the others."

"Paolio."

He turned back. "Yes?"

"I think it would be best if you didn't go mentioning *leprosy* to the others, for the moment."

"You mean Annis." He nodded.

"That's exactly who I mean."

16

WALKABOUT

First officer Annis Romanov felt, rather than heard, the hiss of the main Colony One airlock depressurizing through the thick laminate of her EVA suit. The outer door opened and she stepped out on to the dusty Martian surface. Ahead of her, to the east, lay the ISA HAB module. The others had effectively abandoned it now. With Paolio injured, Decker turned in to a lab rat and Malbec playing nursemaid, the decision had essentially been made for them to relocate to Colony One. After all, it had no shortage of space and food. Nevertheless, it was vital for Annis to establish communications with Earth, and it gave her a valid reason to spend most of her time in the HAB rather than in the contaminated biology of Colony One. She didn't trust the place; the less time spent there the better, as far as she was concerned. Fixing the comms unit was as good a reason as any to isolate herself in the HAB. However, she wasn't going to fix it—she didn't need to. Fortunately she had a plan B. It was part of her mission brief with COM from the very beginning. And now was as good a time as any to execute it.

She looked out across the dunes towards the location of the ISA HAB. Its marker reflected on the heads up display on her visor. Another marker, farther from the HAB, identified the location of the fuel processing plant. And another outlined the Mars lander. This also doubled as the Mars Ascent Vehicle, the MAV. It served both to land on the planet's surface and lift off again to rendezvous with the Odyssey transit craft, still in orbit. To return to Earth they first had to refuel the MAV with supplies from the processing plant. But that operation was a long way off, a few more months at least.

Annis was not heading for the HAB this time. Instead, she took a few paces out from the colony airlock and turned north towards the location of the old supply lander. This had been sent in the aftermath of the disaster, when all contact from Colony One was lost. It contained emergency supplies of food, medicine and survival equipment. There was one item that she had been instructed by COM to utilize once she found an opportune moment early on in the mission. These were instructions to her directly from COM—they were not part of any ISA mission plan.

It was clear to Annis that the mission had already

suffered a major catastrophe with two dead, Paolio injured and Malbec's crazy notion of helping the psychotic Decker. He should have been killed. He was still a danger and no amount of probing and poking by Malbec was going to change that. He had been contaminated by something in the colony and it was only when Annis left that she felt safe. If she had her way, they would leave this godforsaken place now. She was the first officer, the de-facto commander of the mission now that Decker had been compromised. She would not be brushed aside as if she were a minor entity, a bit player.

Annis moved across the dusty crater's surface, picking her way through the detritus of abandoned equipment. Every now and then she would pass the body of a dead colonist, a graphic reminder of the horror that had befallen the great Colony One adventure. After a time she left the main site behind and entered into the solar array field. Hundreds of black panels laid out across the crater, each slightly elevated to catch the maximum amount of sunlight. She looked up. A pale orb hung low in the Martian sky, bathing the solar array with life giving photons. She examined one of the panels. It was remarkably dust free. They had their own self-cleaning system, but they still needed regular manual maintenance to function at optimum levels. And the only way that could happen is if Nills went out onto the planet's surface. "So he *does* EVA." She was beginning to mistrust him even more. She moved on.

It took a full fifteen minutes to get through the array field and arrive at the location of the old supply lander. Its squat form rose out of the landscape like the conning tower of a submarine breaking through the ice. The bright red COM logo emblazoned on the side was still visible. The three and a half years of Martian dust and sand had still not etched it clean.

Annis located the hatch and worked the levers to open it. Once the bolts retracted she grabbed the handles, lifted the entire door off and set it down on the sand. The inside was jammed with equipment and supplies. She started unloading bags and boxes. None of these were of any use to her, what she was looking for was the emergency communications unit.

When this supply mission was being put together, it had been considered that the comms might be damaged, and that any survivors would need a way to communicate with Earth. COM still had its satellite in orbit around the planet, targeted on the colony site. All the comms unit had to do was connect with that satellite and two-way communications could be re-established.

It didn't take her long to find what she was looking for. Two suitcase sized units, one a satellite uplink and the other the comms unit. She dragged them out of the modules and put them down on the ground outside. She then brought up her 3D display and tapped out the commands to call the rover to her location. It would take a few minutes so she repacked the supply module and replaced the outer hatch. Annis then moved the satellite uplink unit to the far side of the supply module so it would not be visible from the colony, unpacked it and extended the solar array. Having spent three years inside the supply module it was unlikely that it had any charge, in fact she was doubtful that it even worked.

She waited. Every now and then she would check the satellite unit to see if it showed any signs of life. She was beginning to think that it was totally dead when the unit responded with an orange charge light. So far so good. After a few more minutes the charge light turned green. *Okay, time to see if this puppy works.* She extended the dish antenna and hit the search button. The unit was now slowly tracking across the sky seeking out the communications satellite, and it didn't take long to find it. The small screen came to life and showed the connection and signal strength. *Excellent,* thought Annis. In about thirty minutes time the old COM control center back on Earth would see the connection.

By the time Annis had finished establishing the satellite link the rover was already in sight, rolling across the surface, tracking to her location. Setting up the satellite link was only half the job. She now needed to unpack and power up the comms unit. Only then could she send a report. This however, could only be done inside. So when the rover finally arrived she threw the unit onto it and headed for the HAB. All going well, she should now be able to re-establish communication with Earth and talk directly to COM, without ISA snooping in on the conversation.

THE CLOSER TO the HAB she got, the less paranoid she felt. It had become her safe zone. A place where she felt insulated from the malignancy of the Colony One environment. She unloaded the comms unit from the back of the rover and entered the airlock. She waited as it repressurized and decontaminated her EVA suit, removing any dust and particles that had accumulated. She wished it would decontaminate her as well. She was beginning to feel like her body was invaded by the contamination from the colony. The light went green and she wasted no time in stripping off her EVA suit before entering the HAB interior. The place was still a mess after Decker had trashed it. She should really clean it up. *Some other time,* she thought. In the operations area she hoisted the unit up onto the bench, opened it up and spent a few minutes connecting power from the central HAB source.

The screen illuminated and showed a schematic of the satellite's position and strength of signal. Everything looked good. Time to send her report. Annis kept it short and to the point, it was done in a few minutes. Nevertheless, it would take at least thirty minutes for it to reach Earth, and at least another hour before COM could digest her message and formulate a reply. She had time to kill, so she decided to take a shower and wash the colony grime from her body.

The prevailing paranoia that rumbled beneath the surface of First Officer Annis Romanov's sanity was one of contamination. If Decker had succumbed to it then maybe it was only a matter of time until they all met the same fate. Yet none of the others had shown any signs of mental instability —at least no more than normal. And Nills said it only infected some. But then a thought struck her as the hot shower beat down on her back. *Maybe he's the one infecting them, maybe he's picking them off one by one—him and that robot sidekick.*

Her arm hurt and she realized that she had been scrubbing it until it was red raw, trying to wash the contamination out of her. She stopped the shower and got out to dry herself. She still didn't feel clean. It was like it was inside her and no amount of scrubbing was going to shift it. She dressed, tied her hair back and went over to the operations area to check on the comms unit. A message had come through. It was direct from Nagle Bagleir and started with the usual bullshit. Annis carefully listened to the message twice, to ensure that she understood what they required of her. When it finished she sat back in the chair, ran her fingers through her still wet hair and laughed. "That crazy hippie's not going to like this."

17

THE ANALOGUE

All had gone dark—again. It looked like Rick Mannersman's premonitions were turning out to be true. There had been no communication with the ISA crew now for over twenty-four hours and anxious eyes in mission control scanned satellite imagery for any clue as to surface activity—there was still hope. Peter VanHoff's tablet pinged and the avatar that was Nagle materialized in front of his field of vision and spoke. "Some interesting developments, Peter."

"This better be good news."

"Good and bad. The good news is our agent, First Officer Annis Romanov, has re-established communications by utilizing the emergency comms unit, sent up on the last supply lander."

"Excellent."

"Indeed, it means we now have direct communications with her, outside the sphere of ISA influence. The bad news is that our worst fears may have been realized."

"Don't tell me... it's happening again."

"I'm afraid so. The ISA Commander Decker has developed a violent and destructive psychosis. So far he has killed Chief Engineer Kevin Novack and Seismologist Lu Chan."

"Oh dear God, no."

"Nonetheless, our agent has seen fit to contain the commander. He is strapped down in the medlab and suitably sedated. She has also set Dr. Malbec the task of establishing the cause."

"Is that wise?"

"Only time will tell. What I do think would be wise is if Romanov redirects any analysis back to us, so we can get some clues as to the nature of this affliction."

"Hmmm. I see. Does ISA know any of this yet?"

"The commander has also destroyed the ISA comms unit in the HAB, hence the reason there have been no reports to ISA. So no, they are still in the dark and we have not informed them, as yet. But there is another significant development. A survivor has been found."

"You're kidding me, after all this time?"

"Nills Langthorp, colonist number thirteen."

"How in God's name did he survive this long?"

"From what we know of him he is a highly skilled engineer and very resourceful."

"Well, I suggest we see how things develop before informing ISA. Because once we do, there goes our control again."

"My thoughts exactly."

"Has Romanov located the *Analogue*?"

"Not yet, the research lab is shutdown. They will need to bring it back online first."

"Can she not EVA in there and retrieve it?"

"Difficult. If the entire facility were derelict then yes, she could. I know that was our initial plan, but the fact that it's not makes the operation risky. We have to make it operational first."

"I don't like it. We can't have them poking around in that lab. Particularly if this Dr. Malbec is involved in the analysis. That lab would be an Aladdin's cave for her."

"It's a risk we have to take if we want the Analogue."

Peter VanHoff paced, a habit of his when he was thinking. He turned back to the avatar that was Nagle. "Fine, if we must. But once the Analogue has been retrieved that lab needs to be destroyed. No one must know what went on in there. Is that understood?"

"Yes. I will instruct Romanov on how to proceed."

"Ensure that she is suitably motivated. She may be

required to go well beyond the initial mission brief before this is over. Particularly if Malbec gets too nosy—or lucky."

"Understood." The avatar that was Nagle extinguished itself.

18

NO RETURN

Jann opened the door to the incubator and inspected the petri dish cultures. One from each of the remaining ISA crew and one from Nills. It was plainly obvious, from the multitude of blots populating the agar gel, that they were all infected. Yet, Jann checked them anyway, one by one, under the microscope just to be certain. And there it was, the same elongated bacterium that had infected Decker, and possibly morphed him into a deranged psychotic. It was present in all the crew samples. However, it was only Decker that had developed the devastating psychological transformation. The good news, if she could call it that, was their infection load was much lower. It seemed that all but Decker had some way of fighting the infection, fending off the biological invasion and keeping them sane.

Nills, on the other hand, was clear. Even though he had been exposed to this for years, his sample looked to Jann to be completely free of the bacteria. Perhaps she made some mistake in preparing it. She would need to check again to be absolutely sure.

The implications of these results began to percolate in Jann's mind. The bacteria were highly virulent and once infected, you either went psychotic or your body figured out a way to live with it. This meant that there was only one option now—she had to find a way to kill it. And if she failed, then none of them could leave the planet. Ever.

The risk of carrying this plague back home and infecting Earth was unthinkable. It had the potential to devastate the human race. A pandemic bordering on apocalypse. Of course, she was assuming that this bacterium was in fact the cause. Jann had no real proof of that—as yet. She looked over at Decker. His chest rose and fell as the monitors drew out his life in luminescent peaks and troughs. He had been lying in stasis for a long time now. His consciousness held in check by the drip-drip of drugs. *How long would he last like that?* she wondered. A month, less? It was slow death by starvation. Perhaps Annis was right. Killing him might have been better —more humane. Yet, she had to try. It had gone beyond simply Decker now, they were all in this, all infected. If she was to ever see the blue planet again then she had to find a solution. A way to kill it.

Since it was a bacterium, it might be as simple as

administering a course of the appropriate antibiotic, as Paolio had suggested. The lab was well stocked, although how much was in date would impact on its effectiveness. But they had others in the HAB. It would help if she knew more about the type of bacteria she was dealing with here. It was engineered, that much she was certain. But how and why she had no clue, unless she could dig deeper into its DNA. For the moment at least, she had no way to perform those kinds of test. Not that it mattered in reality. Decker would be the guinea pig. If the antibiotics worked on him they would work on the rest of them. In the meantime she would repeat the culture test on Nills. If it still proved negative then here at least was a potential source of biological answers—maybe even an antibody. But she was getting ahead of herself.

On the bench, beside the microscope, a red LED blinked on her comms headset. She picked it up, placed over her head and hit the receive button. It was Annis.

"Malbec, nice of you to answer. You'll be happy to hear I managed to re-establish communications with Earth."

"That's great, you fixed it. What was wrong with it?"

"Eh... look I don't have time to get into the technicalities. Suffice to say, I managed to send a report back to Earth."

"And?"

"And the upshot is they want to get the research lab back online. They reckon it will help you in your investigations."

"That's fantastic."

"Now listen. We need to get that hippie on board with this. I've

been sent the boot-up routines and schematics, but it would be better if he and that goofy robot of his help us. He knows the systems better than anyone."

"Okay, when are you coming back here?"

"I'm on my way."

"Well bring some food... and coffee."

"Malbec, we've got more important things to concern ourselves with than food."

"If you want to get Nills on board then there is no better way than to come bearing gifts. He's been living on a diet of fish and plants for years. He may well be in need of a change —even if it's just for the novelty."

"Fine, I get your point."

"And Annis..."

"What?"

"When you get here, be nice."

"Jesus, Malbec. Next you'll be asking me to seduce him with my womanly charms."

I wouldn't worry about that. You don't have any, thought Jann as she switched off the headset.

ANNIS DUTIFULLY BROUGHT BACK SUPPLIES. They consisted of some standard ISA food rations and a few pouches of ground coffee. Nills was tucking into a portion of Chicken Tikka Masala. "This is just amazing. I had forgotten how good it tastes."

"Consider it an Indian takeout, with a 140 million mile delivery," said Paolio. "To be honest, we're pretty tired of it after three months."

"And this coffee is simply ambrosial." He sipped the thick black beverage. "You know, we tried to grow the Arabica plant up here. Not very successfully. It's a difficult and temperamental plant to grow, even on Earth."

"What did mission control have to say?" Jann was prompting Annis to get to the point now that Nills had been softened up.

"They want the research lab brought back online."

Nills stopped eating and looked wide-eyed at Annis. "No way. It's too dangerous. And besides, there's every possibility that none of the equipment will work after all this time."

"Well that's what they want us to do—with or without your help," said Annis.

"What's the difficulty in bringing the research lab back online?" asked Jann.

Nills sighed and sat back in the battered armchair. "There are lots. For one it's a power suck. That's the reason we shut it down back during the storm. It uses a whack load of juice. Two, it's been sitting in deep-freeze for over three years so if things start shorting then it could cause more serious power problems back along the line, jeopardizing the main colony life support. Not something to take lightly."

"But I thought parts of it are still up and running?"

"Yes, there are systems in there still powered up. They

can't be shut down, I don't know why, but they were obviously important."

"We could isolate all the ancillary equipment circuits, use a standalone power source, bring life support up first, then power up the machines one by one as needed," offered Gizmo.

Nills gave him a look as if to say '*traitor*.' He scratched his chin and then poked at the Indian takeout with his fork. "Maybe. But we would still need to recycle the air supply a few times to clean it out while keeping it isolated. That's assuming there are no leaks, you know, that the modules can still hold one atmosphere of pressure. And the condensation buildup doesn't short anything out."

"We have to try. There's probably a lot of specialist equipment in there that might help us find answers to this infection."

"Assuming that's what it is, an infection. Who's to say it not related to the Martian gravity or contamination in the soil or a whole lot of other things?" said Nills.

"What were they doing in there anyway? We've got no record of it in our initial brief. In fact it doesn't even show on anything we have." Jann flicked through a sheaf of ISA notes and diagrams.

"Genetic research, at least that's what they said." Nills was now biting into an apple. He wiped his mouth with the back of his hand, leaned in and looked at them intently. "Four of them... they were a breed apart. They came shortly after the biodome was built and started creating the research lab. Dr. Venji and three others. Said they were developing new bio-organisms for the colony. But there was something about them, kept themselves away from everyone else. They had their own accommodation module, ate their own food, seldom mixed with the rest of us. Rumors started that COM was planning to return them back to Earth after... whatever it was they were doing was finished. I don't know if that's true or not. But one thing is for sure, they were up to lot more than they let on." He sat back and waved the apple core in the air. "To be fair, they did bring a lot of advanced medical equipment and supplies with them." He dumped the apple core into the remains of the Tikka Masala. "About six months into their stay here they started doing tests on all the colonists. Medical checks they called them. They got more frequent as time went on."

"What sort of checks?" said Paolio.

Nills waved his hand. "Checks, I don't know. They would lay us out in the medlab and wire us up. Told us we were in perfect health, and all that."

"We need to get that lab back online, and then maybe we can find some answers," said Jann

"I doubt that any of it will still work." Nills shrugged his shoulders. "But hey... if you think it's worth trying then Gizmo and I will give it a go." He stood up. "We'll have to run a lot of diagnostics first, so that's going to take a bit of time."

"How long?"

"I don't know, several hours at least. Then we can try. But first, I have other work to attend to. What with all these extra mouths to feed." He got up and moved off towards the biodome, Gizmo following faithfully behind.

PAOLIO SIPPED HIS COFFEE. "He's probably right, you know."

"About what?"

"About none of the equipment functioning."

"Maybe." Jann wondered if now would be a good time to break the news. "I've done some preliminary tests on our blood samples."

"And?" said Annis, sitting forward.

"I've found traces of the same bacteria in Decker in all of us."

"Shit," said Annis. "You mean we're all infected?"

"Except for Nills. He seems to be clear, as far as I can tell."

"I knew it. Don't you see, he's infecting us?" Annis was standing up pointing back in the direction of the biodome.

"That's crazy. He's just built up an immunity to it. He probably doesn't even know himself." Jann was now also standing, facing off with Annis.

Annis seemed to back off a bit. "Maybe, but I still don't trust him." She started to pace. "Do you know what it is?"

Jann hesitated, she wasn't sure how Annis was going to react. "It's a genetically modified variant of *Mycobacterium Leprae.*"

"What the hell is that?"

"Leprosy," said Paolio.

"Leprosy? You mean this is a goddamn leper colony?"

"No, it's a derivative, not the same thing."

"So how do you get rid of it? Annis was leaning into the table now.

"We're trying some antibiotics, but none have worked so far," said Paolio.

"Well that's just great, just goddamn great." She sat down again shaking her head.

"It's impossible to know with what we've got in the medlab, Annis," said Paolio. "That's why we need the research lab up and running."

"There's one other thing," said Jann. She might as well get it all out on the table, so to speak.

"What now?" said Annis.

"We can't leave this planet until we find a cure."

Annis was back on her feet again. "That's bullshit."

"No, seriously, we can't afford to bring this back to Earth."

"No way, I'm not staying on this rock any longer than I have to. I didn't sign up for this crap." She was moving around, waving her hands in the air. "Screw this," she said, and stormed out of the common room.

JANN AND PAOLIO SAT in silence for a minute.

"I thought she took that pretty well, all things considered." Paolio said finally.

"Where's she off to? Back to the HAB?"

"I'll talk to her later, once she settles down a bit."

"She's losing it," said Jann.

"She's just under a lot of stress, we all are."

"There's one other thing," said Jann.

"I'm not sure if I can take any more. What now?"

"It's Annis. Her infection load is much higher than the rest of us."

Paolio picked up his coffee cup from the table and looked over at Jann. "You think she's a risk?"

"I don't know. It's nowhere near Decker's, but it's much higher that than rest of us."

Paolo looked into his empty cup. "I think I'm going to need a lot of strong coffee." He swung his wheelchair in the direction of the galley.

"I'd better go and talk to Nills." Jann stood up and headed for the biodome.

Paolio turned back to her with a smile, "Oh, and Jann..."

"What?"

"Remind me never to have dinner with you ever again."

19

BIO-DOME

Jann went in search of Nills and found him deep inside the biodome. He was in an area where he had created the garden, as he liked to call it. It was a rustic vegetable patch, no hydroponics, no hi-tech lab equipment, no use of any twenty-first century technology. Of course, this belied the fact that all plants were bioengineered, the soil was treated with specially manufactured GM bacteria to cleanse it of Martian toxins and no pests would ever come to blight this crop. Nevertheless, it had the outward appearance of a typical kitchen garden, an oasis of low-tech simplicity in an environment of hi-tech engineering.

He was digging potatoes and piling them into containers. His fluid movements told of long practice at this very task. Jann watched him for a while from a distance, peering through the gaps in the overgrowth. His simple unhurried movements had a calming effect on her. Eventually, it was he that spoke first. "I won't bite, you know."

"Sorry, I didn't mean to spy." She came out from behind a large hanging vine. He stopped and rested an arm on the handle of his spade and gave her a bright smile. If it hadn't been for the latticework of the domed roof in the background he looked just like any artisan gardener, working in his allotment back on Earth.

"Want to help? It's good for the spirit."

Jann considered this for a moment. Paolio was talking to Annis, getting her head straightened out—hopefully. Decker was going nowhere and there was not much else she could do until the research lab was brought back online. "Sure, why not."

"Here, let me show you." He picked up a short handled fork. "You dig in like this, not too hard, so you don't skewer a spud. Then lift out the earth and give it a shake." Four potatoes of varying sizes were resting on the fork. He leaned over to pick one up. "These bigger ones we store for eating, these smaller ones go into this container and we'll keep them for replanting." He handed her the fork. "Think you can manage it?"

"Hey, you're talking to a farm girl here. I grew up tending vegetables." She took the fork and went to work. Nills was right, it was good for the spirit. After a while they got into a rhythm. Nills went ahead and pulled up plants as Jann followed by digging out tubers. They harvested quite a bit in the time they were at it.

"Okay, I think that's enough for now." He wiped the sweat from his forehead. "Let's get these stored." They carried the boxes between them as they traversed the biodome over to a processing room. It was small and crammed with machines, most of which seemed to be of Nills' own making. They laid the boxes on a long bench. Jann watched him as he fiddled with one of the contraptions and started it up.

"Did you ever get lonely up here, all those years on your own?"

"Yea, sure. Well... at first there were three of us, after we got rid of the last crazy."

"What happened to them?" Jann continued, now that Nills was ready to talk again.

"Jonathan... died of natural causes, not sure what exactly. He simply wasted away over a few months. It was hard to watch him go like that, after all he'd been through. That left myself and Bess."

"Bess? Bess Keilly?"

"Yes, did you know her?"

"No. We... eh... came across her... body, in the stone hut, out past the big dune."

Nills stopped sorting the potatoes and hung his head. He said nothing for a while, then spoke in a soft tone, almost a whisper. "So that's where she went. I should have known." He looked up at Jann again. "We were close. But the isolation began to get to her. She became more and more depressed as each day passed. Eventually, she just went out the airlock one morning and never came back."

"Oh... I'm sorry, I didn't mean to..."

Nills shrugged. "It's okay."

After a moment Jann continued. "Did you ever try to look for her?"

"Yes, but I started to get panic attacks when I went EVA. They got worse and worse each time I went out. Eventually I just stopped trying."

"So that's why you don't go outside?"

"Yeah. Fortunately Gizmo can go out for me if something really needs to be done, like cleaning the solar panels, that sort of stuff."

"It must have been hard on you."

He waved a hand. "Ah... it's just this place, what happened, everything. It tries very hard to kill you, one way or the other. Physically, mentally, emotionally.

"Do you ever miss Earth?"

"In the beginning I did. But after a while I realized what I really missed was the physical Earth, the natural beauty of it. What I didn't miss was humanity's desire to destroy it." He turned back to the machine and adjusted some dials. "But tell me... would you miss Earth?"

Jann sighed. "If I don't find an answer to this infection then I don't think we'll be going home. So, ask me again if we're still here in a few months."

"Ahh, I see. Sorry if I don't look surprised. I could have told you that the first time we met." He proceeded to empty the harvested potatoes into a hopper on the machine and started it up. It made a horrendous racket. He signaled to Jann with a nod of his head to move back into the biodome. Jann waited until they were in a quiet spot before telling him her news. "I've run some tests on the blood samples we took. We're all infected, except you."

He stopped. "I see. Do you know what it is?"

"I think your hunch was right, it's caused by a bacterial infection."

"And you say I don't have it?"

"No, not as far as I can tell, but I need to do more tests to be certain."

Nills considered this for a moment. "You know, this all started to happen after the research lab was in operation."

"Is that why you don't want to reactivate it?"

"What do you think? Whatever is in that lab doesn't need to get out again."

"But if that's where it came from then we may have a chance of finding out what it is... and maybe find a way to kill it."

Nills scratched his chin again, like he couldn't get used to not having a beard. He had shaved it off a while ago and it made him look even younger. Jann and the others still couldn't quite get over his youthful appearance. Paolio had put it down to diet. He also postulated that maybe the one-third gravity had a beneficial effect on aging. But this was all speculation. Nonetheless, Nills looked like a twenty year old, not someone the wrong side of thirty-five.

"If it's bacteria then surely antibiotics would kill it?"

"We've been trying various types on Decker's samples, but still no luck. It seems to be highly resistant to anything we've thrown at it so far."

"Like it was engineered that way?" He stopped and looked at her.

"Yes, that's what I'm beginning to think. We're dealing with something that was engineered rather than evolved here. You have to remember that bacteria can evolve relatively fast. I had thought that it was something designed for the ecosystem here that had mutated."

"But now you're not so sure?"

"No. That's why we need to get into the research lab and take a look."

As if on cue, Gizmo sped into the biodome. "Nills, I've done the diagnostics and run through a number of activation sequences. My best scenario has a 78% success probability."

"Thanks, Gizmo." He turned back to Jann. "Are you sure you want to do this?"

"Yes, it's the only option… if we're ever going to be able to return to Earth."

"It's not so bad here. After a few years you might even get to like it." He laughed.

Jann smiled and looked around her. He did have a point,

even if he was just joking. It had a beauty to it, like an oasis in a world gone mad, even if that oasis was 140 million miles away. "Yeah, I might."

"Although it's better when you have someone to share it with." He smiled and at that moment Jann found herself quite attracted to this enigmatic soul. He radiated calm and serenity and Jann felt herself drawn in by its glow. She stopped short and looked away. "I should go and check in with Paolio, see how the commander is doing. Maybe he has some good news with the antibiotics."

"Okay, sure. Gizmo and I need to... eh, run through some more stuff, anyway. If everything checks out then we'll start reactivation tomorrow."

"Great." She walked out of the garden, heading for the medlab.

HER MEETING with Nills had left Jann feeling more optimistic, or maybe she was just less pessimistic. Either way she no longer had a tight knot of apprehension in her gut. She decided not to go and find Paolio just yet. He might still be talking to Annis and she didn't want to interrupt that dialogue. Instead, Jann sat down in the common area on a battered armchair and took some time out.

Along the wall were pinned a number of sketches and artworks, presumably created by the colonists, back in happier times. They all depicted scenes from Mars. Some were landscapes, some portraits of people, some were even quite accomplished. One caught her eye. It was a well crafted landscape sketched with some type of brown charcoal. In the foreground two colonists in full EVA suits embraced. She stared at it for a while.

What was the worst thing that could happen? They would be stranded here. Was that so bad? Jann began to think the unthinkable and the more she thought about it the more she began to feel giddy. Was it so strange to imagine a life in a botanical paradise, shared with the radiant Nills? She shook her head, she was getting soppy. But then again, if this was worst case scenario, it wasn't so bad after all, at least not in her mind. But what of the others? Paolio and Annis?

Yet there was something else she was not considering in all of this. What was it? Jann couldn't put her finger on it. It was there in her subconscious trying to get out, a new danger, a deeper threat. There was something she was missing. The knot returned in her gut and gripped it tight. Was it the infection, malignly working away to undermine her sanity? A shiver ran through her body. The thought of it repulsed her and dispelled any romantic notions she had of this place. Then another thought exploded in her mind. Could she end up like Decker? A deranged homicidal maniac? "Oh dear God, don't let me lose my mind."

. . .

"Jann." Paolio buzzed into the common room on his motorized wheelchair. "Did you speak to Nills?"

"Yes, he thinks they can start the reactivation of the research lab tomorrow."

"Good."

"How's Annis?"

"She's returned to the HAB."

"Why won't she stay here? We really need to stick together."

"I know, but there was no stopping her. Anyway, I've given her all the data from our sample analysis. She's going to send it through to mission control tonight. Maybe the boffins back on Earth can shed some light on what it is."

"And Decker?"

"The same. No change."

Jann sighed and slumped back in the chair. It was late and she was exhausted. They sat in silence for a moment. Then Jann leaned forward and spoke very low. "Paolio. I want you to do me a favor."

"Sure, name it."

"If... if I should go like Decker, you know... succumb to this infection. I want you to... kill me."

"Jesus, Jann, that's a bit dramatic... anyway, it's not going to happen."

"But if it does, you promise me you'll do this."

"It's not going to come to that."

"Promise me."

Paolio looked at her for a moment. "You know I can't promise that. I'm a doctor. My duty is to save life, not end it."

Jann slumped back in her chair again. "I'm sorry, I shouldn't have asked you, it's unfair of me." She looked back at the wall of paintings. "Maybe you're right. Maybe it won't come to that."

"Let's hope not."

20

RECALIBRATION

Nills examined the rows of overripe tomatoes. Some had already fallen from the vine and would be good for nothing except composting. He should have picked them at least three days ago. The beans needed tying up and he really should check the herb garden to see which plants had seeds ready to save. His carefully scheduled tasks were falling behind and now he was playing catch up. The arrival of the ISA crew had thrown a spanner into his world and created stress where before there was harmony. The rhythm that he and Gizmo had grown accustomed to was disrupted. A new dynamic had entered colony life and new demands were being placed on its resources. Deep down, he knew this would happen sooner or later. New people would come to investigate what had happened, or simply tempted by the lure of adventure. Still, it was good to be able to talk to another human. For a long time he was uncertain of his own sanity. Had he gone mad after all these years? That uncertainty had been put to rest now, as he had truly survived—with his mind intact.

He thought of Jann, or was it Bess? He shook his head. He needed more time, it was too soon to contemplate such emotions. "Put it out of your mind," he said to himself.

"Put what out of your mind?" said Gizmo, who was shadowing him as he worked.

"Oh, nothing, I was just thinking aloud," he said as he snipped a bunch of tomatoes and placed it in a box that Gizmo was holding for him. He stopped for a moment, looked around him and considered what he had achieved here in those three and a half long years.

In the beginning, the agriculture at Colony One had been utilitarian. Scientifically calculated to maximize yields. The plants where the vegetative equivalent of battery hens. The biodome was a factory simply for producing food. But since the demise of the colony population high yields had become unnecessary, so Nills had set about creating more of a garden than a factory. Slowly but surely he had given over more space to his Eden. And slowly but surely it gave him purpose and fortified his spirit. He would sit for long hours, surrounded by the lush vegetation, listening to the sound of the water flowing in the pond and stare up through the dome roof into the nighttime sky. It was at these moments that he realized you can take the human out of the Earth but you can't take the Earth out of the human. He might be living on an alien planet, but all around him was the very essence of Earth, of nature itself, of what it meant to be a living creature. He was more in tune with the ecosystem on this dusty godforsaken rock than he ever had been back home. It had taken him 140 million miles to get back to the garden.

He wiped a bead of sweat from his brow with his sleeve and set to work again. Both he and Gizmo spent their time harvesting and tending to the tomatoes as these were the most urgent. Then Nills turned his attention to building up the soil around a newly sprouting crop of potatoes as Gizmo went off to store the night's harvest. The little robot returned just as Nills finished the last of his work.

"They are related, you know."

"Who are?" replied Gizmo.

"Tomatoes and potatoes. They're both from the nightshade family, which includes *Deadly Nightshade*, a highly toxic plant."

"Interesting. I will make a note of that. Perhaps it may be a useful tidbit to regurgitate when I am next put upon in polite company, and find myself wanting for a fascinating fact to toss into the conversation."

Nills cocked an eyebrow and the little robot. "Indeed," he replied. "I think we're done here for tonight, Gizmo."

"The strawberries are sprouting new runners, should we not get these staked down?"

"Time enough for that tomorrow. There's been too much

excitement around our little garden these last couple of days."

"Yes, it has been a rather dramatic interlude."

"I'm tired now. Come, let's sit a while and talk." Nills put away his garden tools and walked into the center of the dome. The little robot whirred along beside him. He sat down on a low chair fashioned from wood he had pruned from the fruit trees in the biodome over the years. It had a rustic artisanal look and felt perfectly in keeping with the verdant surroundings. Beside it was a low table made from the same materials. Nills waved his hand over the holo-tab that was resting there. A three dimensional control interface rendered itself above the surface and he tapped several of the icons in quick succession. A series of screens materialized, showing charts and data of the colony systems. Nills studied them for a while. "I see you have compensated for the additional oxygen requirement, Gizmo."

"Yes, Nills. Several adjustments needed to be made to accommodate the additional Earthlings."

"Very good. Everything looks nominal."

"I would suggest we need to recalibrate our food production process at some point. They could eat us out of house and home."

Nills scratched his chin. "This is a concern. However, they *have* brought their own supplies. Enough for a hundred days I understand. Since two are dead and one incapacitated then this could stretch for longer. So that gives us some time to increase our planting."

"Do they know yet that they will not be returning to Earth?" said Gizmo.

"It is only beginning to dawn on them. The problem will be how they are going to react when they do finally realize."

"Will they be disappointed?"

"Hopefully it's just disappointment and nobody starts getting crazy—doing something stupid."

"Yes, that would be most unfortunate."

Nills was now looking at a recording from one of the many cameras in the biodome. It was from a few hours earlier and showed Annis Romanov jogging around the path along the inner wall. She was panting and pushing hard. He studied her face as it swept into full view; he paused it. "We need to keep a close eye on her, Gizmo."

"Is she dangerous?"

"Unpredictable. And we don't like that do we?" He turned and looked at the robot.

"No, we like a place for everything, and everything in its place."

"Exactly." He returned to the screen and tapped another icon. The recording of Romanov extinguished and was replaced by a direct video feed from the accommodation module. It was of a naked Dr. Jann Malbec preparing to have a shower. Nills flinched, his finger hovered over the camera control to switch it off and not intrude—but he lingered. He was drawn by the beauty of her poise, the arc of her neck, the curve of her spine. A memory stirred within him.

"Is she dangerous, too?" said Gizmo.

Nills tapped the off icon. "No, no, she's just... never mind." Nills' head slumped and he looked at the ground for quite some time before reaching up to wipe a tear from his eye.

Gizmo moved closer to his master and spoke in a surprisingly low tone. "Is it Bess again? Your eyes always water when you think of her."

Nills cocked a smile and the quirky robot. "Yes, Gizmo, I miss her and... well, she reminds me of her." He wiped his face again, shook his head and tapped another icon. This time a feed from the medlab showed Paolio examining the stricken Decker. Nills sat back in his chair and watched it for a while. From a pocket in his flight suit he took out a small metal box. He carefully opened it up and proceeded to roll himself a joint. He lit it, took a long drag and settled himself back into the wicker recliner. He watched the doctor take a blood sample from the commander and prepare it for more tests.

"Gizmo."

"Yes Nills."

"I think tomorrow it's time to give you an upgrade."

"Excellent, what sort of upgrade?"

"I think maybe a weapon or two might come in handy."

"Splendid, I do love playing with new gadgets."

21

LIES

Peter VanHoff scanned the lab report sent by first officer Romanov in her most recent communication. It was a blood sample analysis done by Dr. Jann Malbec on the ISA crew and the sole colonist Nills Langthorp. It was Malbec's identification of the bacterial infection that interested him most. He was impressed. It was clear that his geneticists on Colony One had been busy, as this was evidently their work. What intrigued him, however, was the fact that Nills Langthorp showed no signs of the infection. And what made this even more interesting was Romanov's observation of his youthful appearance. Clearly then, this bacteria had been an earlier attempt. They had come close, but the side effects were disastrous. He put the report aside, stood up, and paced.

The intention had always been to return the science

team. There was only so much that could be done remotely. Although that turned out to be quite a lot. Nevertheless, acquisition of the active biology was the end game. The other reason was that it was difficult to get a team with any depth assembled if the mission was one-way. They just wouldn't go. But offer a return mission and then COM would have its pick of the best talent. They had been working on developing their own return mission for quite some time. But all that stopped when the colony fell apart. And with no more money coming in, it was left to wither on the vine. Getting into bed with ISA had been the only option left.

He waved a hand over the holo-tab and touched the icon to summon his second in command. A few moments later the avatar that was Nagle materialized in Peter VanHoff's field of vision and spoke.

"Good evening, Peter. How are you feeling today?"

"I told you not to keep asking me that."

"It's just a greeting, nothing more."

Peter grunted. "Have you seen the infection loads in the report?"

"I have."

"The survivor Nills Langthorp is clean."

"I noticed that, very interesting."

"This is all the evidence we need. I suggest we move forward our plans."

"I concur. I have also come to the conclusion that the

mental state of our agent is deteriorating. At this rate we may not get another chance."

"Yes, I did notice her load was higher than the others, barring the commander of course. How is she holding up?"

"So far, so good. But that status may change very quickly the longer she is exposed. She is becoming more paranoid of Langthorp and the colony in general. She keeps referring to it as a leper colony. Also, Malbec is trying to convince her that returning to Earth would be catastrophic."

"Yes, well it would be—if we were going to let her live."

"My thoughts exactly. So I think we need to act now to secure the Analogue and complete the mission."

"You have a plan then?"

"Yes, it is as simple as it is elegant. Fortunately, Romanov's current state leaves her exposed to straightforward psychological manipulation. In essence, I plan to lie."

"Excellent. It's time to bring home the bacon, then."

ANNIS PACED the HAB floor with a deep primal rhythm, back and forth, back and forth, back and forth. She waited out time in measured steps. Each one closer to a reply from Earth. It should come soon.

The comms unit chimed an alert. A message had arrived. Annis broke her step, wheeled towards the unit and tapped receive. The avatar that was Nagle materialized before her and shimmered like a fiery beacon, a light in the darkness of an alien world. It spoke...

'We understand your concern, first officer Romanov, and concur with your hypothesis that the colonist, Nills Langthorp, is in fact the cause of this infection. We have long suspected that he may have even instigated the collapse of the colony. From Dr. Malbec's analysis, which you sent back in your report, we have ascertained that he, and the rest of your crew, are now all contaminated with a highly malign form of leprosy. However, you may remember the inoculations that our medical team administered to you before you departed. These were to provide a certain level of biological protection. Suffice to say, they are working and fortunately you are not contaminated—thus far. Nevertheless, the longer you stay on the planet the less effective this protection will be and your life will be in increasing danger.

Therefore, it is imperative that you acquire the Analogue now and prepare the MAV for your return to Earth. You must also ensure all contaminants have been eradicated by destroying the research lab. Forsake all thoughts of the others as they can no longer be saved. You must save yourself. You are all that is left of the mission. We have the utmost faith in your ability to fulfill this difficult operation and return to Earth with the Analogue.

Good luck and God speed.'

The avatar that was Nagle faded and extinguished itself. In its place was left an empty space that was now being filled with the frenetic thoughts of First Officer Annis Romanov. *Return to Earth, leave the others, destroy the colony? Did she hear that right?* She paced over and across the HAB floor, bisecting it in a steady even pace, all the time thinking on the new mission requirements. She was not contaminated—Malbec was lying. She could still get out of this alive, and she could get out now.

Assuming that the research lab came back online, acquiring the Analogue would be simple. Preparing the MAV for launch without alerting the others would be a much more difficult task. What she needed was a distraction in Colony One, something to keep them all busy and buy her enough time. She required around thirty minutes to prepare the craft, another hour to move the six fuel canisters from the manufacturing plant and attach them, then another twenty minutes or so to run the prelaunch diagnostic. Around two hours in all.

She moved into the HAB airlock and donned her EVA suit. Time to head back to Colony One, hopefully for the last time. She closed her visor and hit the button for the outer door. Once the pressure was equalized she stepped out on to the surface and walked towards the seismic rover, its surface already covered in a layer of dust. From the rear storage hatch she extracted four explosive charges and placed them into a pocket in the front of her suit. "This should be enough of a distraction."

22

RESEARCH LAB

Nills and Gizmo were in the operations area studying a three-dimensional schematic of the research lab systems. They had been working on it all morning. Each time they tried to power up the lab, fail-safe circuits would kick in and power would die. And each time they would analyze the results and try to isolate the problems. Nills zoomed in on one of the four modules attached to the main research lab. "This seems to be the problem area, something in there is tripping the power every time we try and boot up."

"If my analysis of the circuitry is correct, and it generally is, then I would have to postulate that it already has some power," said Gizmo.

"Well, we've known for a long time that the main lab has

been using a little power... for something, God knows what. But this is new." Nills looked over at his robotic friend. For a long time his careful husbandry of Colony One resources concluded that the facility used more power than he could account for. He made many attempts to identify this anomaly, to no avail. In the end he and Gizmo simply factored it into their calculations and lived with it. "Could this be the source of the power suck we've been seeing all this time?"

"I think you could be right. It is consistent with the 2.1% additional power loss we have been calculating."

"It's no wonder we couldn't find it. What the hell is going on in there?"

"Something so important that required it to be integrated with the low level life support. Something they did not want switched off."

Nills looked back at the schematic and drew his finger along a circuit line, pointing out the power connections to Gizmo. "I think we need to disable here and here, and reroute through here. Then we can try life support again."

"Roger that, Captain," said Gizmo. "Reconfiguring circuits now—ready."

"Okay, here goes." Nills tapped a few icons on the table and full power was again routed to the research lab. The schematic lit up with a series of red alerts all across the power circuits. "Shit. Well that didn't work. We're still getting a lot of shorts. I suppose it's to be expected with a unit as complex as this lying in deep-freeze for the last three and a half years. Gizmo, can you identify the new problem area?"

"Working on it." Circuits on the schematic flashed and danced as Gizmo reconfigured lab systems and rerouted connections. This went on for quite a while. "Okay," it said. "Try it again."

This time no alerts flashed. "Looking good, Gizmo. I think you've done it. Modules two and five are running hot, though—wait, looks like they're stabilizing.

"I estimate with the current power consumption we would have thirty five hours and forty six minutes of supply from the remote power unit we've set up," said Gizmo.

"Very good, let start with repressurizing the area." A graphic sea of illuminated bar graphs appeared over each module on the 3D holo-table. They all started to drift upwards and the research lab received its first taste of air in over forty months. The atmosphere now cycled through air scrubbers as they worked to clean it of moisture and contaminants. "Looks like we have a minor integrity issue in number four. Can we compensate?"

"We would have less than two point three percent deterioration over one full sol."

"I think we can live with that." Nills looked at the stats that were now streaming in. "Okay, it's going to take a few hours to cycle enough air through the lab before we can enter."

"Three point three two five, to be exact."

"Okay, you can let it roll. We'll check back on it later. Come, let's get back to the garden."

"Roger that," replied Gizmo.

A LITTLE OVER three hours later, Jann and Paolio were in front of the research lab door as Nills entered the code to open it. "Well, here goes."

They heard a thump as the locking bolts retracted followed by a slight hiss as the door opened forward. Nills stood back and waved his arm. "It's all yours." Jann stepped in first, followed by Paolio. The main lab was a large circular domed space, with racks for scientific equipment lined up along the walls. The center was crisscrossed with workbenches. A ring of pale green light illuminated the area, giving it a strange alien feel.

"There seems to be a lot missing," said Jann. There were obvious gaps both on the floor and in the racks where nothing remained except for a bunch of wires and tubes. Jann crouched down and examined the floor where one such unit was no longer. "Look, you can see the indents where something heavy stood here." She stood up. "Where has all this equipment gone?"

"I know they took some over to the mine," said Nills.

"But so much? More than half the equipment is gone," said Jann. "What were they doing over there?"

Nills just shrugged. "Mining?"

"Look at this." Jann ran her hand along the surface of a large machine, still bolted to the lab floor. "A DNA Sequencer. If this works it could prove very useful."

Around the perimeter of the research lab dome a number of additional modules had been attached, and Nills and Gizmo were examining the door into one of these. She could sense there was something about this module by the way they were discussing it. While Nills fiddled with the door keypad, Jann came over.

"What's in here?"

"It's an anomaly, it still had power going to it." He looked over at her. "It was never offline." Nills had taken apart the keypad, wire spooled out as he probed its innards with a small screwdriver. They heard a thump, and the door unlocked. "Okay, let's go check it out."

Bright fluorescent lights flickered on as they entered. Around the walls were what looked like server racks. Column after column, arrayed side by side all around the circular room. Each column had maybe twenty or so pizza-box sized units stacked horizontally, one on top of the other.

"Looks like a datacenter." Jann examined a unit, running her finger along the cryptic identification number on the slim fascia. She heard a click and jumped back as the unit silently slid out from its housing, the top gracefully opening as it moved. They gathered around and gazed into its mysterious interior. Inside, a myriad of strange illuminated circuitry, rendered in glass or some crystalline plastic, shimmered and pulsed with a slow hypnotic rhythm.

"What's this, some sort of bio-server?" said Paolio.

"Yes, you could say that," said Jann. "It's a biological analogue. A combination of electronic and living circuits— see here and here." Jann pointed to different areas of the strange circuit board. "Each of these sections are a facsimile of different organs: lungs, liver, kidneys. And here, look, the heart... see how it pulsates.

"Incredible."

"They're generally used for drug testing." Jann moved back and pushed the front of another of the units. It slid out and opened, just like the first. "As you know, drug testing is an enormously expensive exercise, and that's before it even gets to human trials. So if you could test a drug on an analogue then a pharmaceutical company could potentially save billions."

"I've heard of these, they've been talked about in medical circles for years. I always thought they were just fantasy." Paolio pushed another one out and was peering into its innards.

"So they were drug testing, that's how they got so much investment."

"More than that, they were doing human DNA engineering." Nills was pushing open more units and peering in. "We suspected it but, they were so secretive about what went on in here, it was mostly just speculation."

Jann suddenly realized. "Oh my God—they're human—they're colonists."

Paolio looked around at the panorama of racks, "There's a lot missing. Look at all these empty spaces. Still, there must be hundreds here. But there were only, what... fifty odd colonists?"

"There's probably at least three or four for each colony member. One would be a control, and could be used to create a genetic replica for experimentation."

"How would they even create such things?" said Paolio.

"Biopsy samples."

"But they would have to slice open all the colonists."

"Or stem cells." Jann looked over at Paolio as they both felt a piece of the puzzle fall into place.

"Stem cells, of course. The bacterium is how they created them. My God."

They all stood for a while just looking around, taking in the horror of what this room represented.

"You're probably in here somewhere." Jann said after a while as she looked over at Nills.

"Yes, but which one? We would need to get the IT systems up and running first to find out. But I don't suppose it matters that much now anyway."

Jann pushed the units back in. "It does if we want to find out what has afflicted the commander, and how to kill it."

"Gizmo's working on getting some of the IT up and running soon. We'll have a better idea then."

Jann's headset beeped. She touched the side of the unit to receive—it was Annis. "Yes."

"*Malbec, any word on that research lab yet?*"

"It's open for business, mostly. You'll never believe what they were doing in here."

"*I'm sure I won't. Anyway you can tell me when I get there. I'm on my way.*"

"Did mission control come back with anything useful?"

"*Eh... no, nothing yet. See you there in a while.*" She shut off her comms unit.

"Annis?" asked Paolio.

"Yeah."

"Any update?"

"None. She'll be here shortly."

"Wonderful." He gave a wry smile.

OVER THE NEXT few hours Nills and Gizmo worked to restore function to various systems within the lab. Jann's priority now was the IT system, or at least what was left of it. The lab had been stripped of much of its equipment, moved to the mine according to Nills. *For what purpose?* she wondered. Not that it mattered for what she wanted to do; there was still a good deal of scientific apparatus remaining, enough for her purposes.

And with access to the IT systems, she might be able to gain some insight into the experiments that had been pursued by COM geneticists. But restoring power to this was proving problematic. So she remained in the research lab to assist Nills and Gizmo. Paolio retired to the medlab to monitor Decker; he had been concerned over his physical state. Annis had still not shown up.

Paolio checked the patient. His chest rose and fell with a steady rhythm. His vitals all looked strong. The cuts and bruises he had acquired were all healed. If Paolio didn't know better, he would think the commander was as healthy as a pig. He spent some time checking the adhesion of the ECG pads on Decker. Then moved on to the drip. He made up a new batch and replaced the old one—it was nearly out. *Wouldn't be good to let that run dry.* He thought about increasing the flow rate but decided to do a quick inventory first. They only had a limited supply of the drug that was keeping Decker subdued. How long would it last? He jotted down some quick calculations on a pad. Twelve days. Not much time to find a cure. And then what?

Decker twitched. Paolio jumped. "Jesus." He moved over to examine the readouts again. Then he took out a penlight and shone it into the commander's pupils, one at a time. He sat back. There was no doubt that Decker was growing stronger, not weaker. The current rate of drug flow was just enough to keep him under and no more. Should he increase it? If he did then this would just shorten the timeline for a more permanent solution. In the end he decided to leave it for the moment. He would check back later and decide then.

BY THE TIME Annis finally showed up it was late. They were all gathered around the table in the common room when Gizmo alerted them to activity in the airlock. Annis arrived carrying a bag. "Evening Annis, glad you could make it. What's in the bag?" said Paolio.

"Eh... I've decided to stay here from now on. I think it's best we all stick together."

Jann gave Paolio a glance. She was skeptical but maybe she should cut Annis some slack. "Come, join us. There's food here if you're hungry."

"No... thanks. I'm fine. Is the research lab operational?"

"Yeah, partly."

"I'm going to have a look." She walked off to investigate. The others followed her with their eyes as she left the common room.

"Don't," said Paolio to Jann.

Jann raised her hands. "I didn't say anything."

"No, but I know what you're thinking. Just let it ride. She's trying, okay?"

"Sure, fine." Jann bit her lip.

Nills stood up. "I need to get back to the garden. I'll show you where she can stay tonight."

"Just make sure it's far away from me," said Jann.

Paolio looked at her.

Jann raised her hands. "Sorry, couldn't help it. It just came out."

23

XFJ-001B

Annis considered the face of Commander Robert Decker as he lay unconscious on the medlab operating table. In the harsh glow of her flashlight she could see he was damp with sweat and flushed with fever as the infection raged inside him. She moved closer and leaned over the bed to inspect the injuries he had sustained to his forehead. They were all healed, and not a scratch remained. "Weird," she thought. She swept the narrow light along the wires that trailed from his body and into the machines that monitored his vital signs. She was about to disconnect them when she hesitated, they might set off an alarm if the status changed. *Best leave them. He can yank them out himself later,* she thought. What she was looking for was the pump that kept him supplied with sedative. The drug delivery system that stopped him from becoming conscious, and kept his violence suppressed. She found it and gently pulled it out of his neck. How long it would take for him to return to consciousness she wasn't sure, an hour, two hours? It was hard to tell. All she knew was that when he did, all hell would break loose. His body twitched and she jumped back in fright. She held her hand over her mouth to suppress any noise she might inadvertently make. She stood and watched him for a few seconds. Maybe he would wake sooner than she thought. "Better get moving, no time to waste."

Annis moved silently out of the medlab and picked her way across the common room floor. It was the middle of the night, 4:35am Mars time. Colony One was in darkness and all the others were asleep. Even Gizmo was docked in his recharge station in the operations room. Still, she couldn't be one hundred percent sure that the robot was totally offline and not monitoring some low level processes. She made her way to the research lab, tiptoeing as she went. The heavy boots of her EVA suit made hard work of keeping silent. The door was open and power was still on. *Good,* she thought. *This will make things quicker.* She scanned the dim interior with her flashlight and made her way to the racks in the module at the far end. These were the *analogues* and it was one of them that she was now searching for, sweeping her flashlight up and down the racks looking for the serial number that COM had given her. This was the *source analogue* that they so desired. Why they wanted it was of no concern to Annis. Other than it was her ticket off this planet. Her flashlight stopped over XFJ-001B. She pressed a button on the fascia and the unit slid out. She grabbed the sides, slid it out of its shelf and placed it carefully inside a rugged case. She thought she heard a noise and stopped, silence. It was just the creaking of the superstructure adjusting to the nighttime temperature.

From the front pocket of her EVA suit she took out one of the seismic charges and set the timer to its maximum. That should be around forty-five minutes. She wedged it in a gap between the racks. She set two more to take out the rest of the units. The last charge she placed against the exterior hull of the lab module. It would be more than enough to open the whole place up like a can of tomatoes in a microwave. "That should keep them busy for a while."

THE STEADY ORANGE LED on Gizmo's breast panel flicked green as he detached himself from the docking station. He spun around and whirred off at full speed to wake Nills. He found him lying in his hammock in the center of the biodome. One arm hung over the side, his hand hovering above a half smoked joint that was poised on the edge of an ashtray fashioned from a small rover dish antenna. Gizmo stroked Nills' arm gently with his metal hand. "Nills, wake up." His eyes snapped open. "Gizmo, what is it?"

"An Earthling has just operated the airlock."

Nills sat up in the hammock and jumped down. "Who?"

"Temperature coefficient of the accommodation modules indicates that First Officer Annis Romanov is not at home."

Nills was now checking the camera feeds on his holo-tab. He flicked through each of the modules. Annis' bed was empty. "What the hell is she up to?"

"I'm afraid I have no logical answer. Perhaps she couldn't sleep and decided to go for a walk."

"Come, let's find out where she is." They moved off together to the operations room.

Dust swirled around Dr. Jann Malbec and engulfed her. It billowed and blew with a frenzy and blocked all sight. It formed into bacteria and they moved and shifted across her field of vision. She thought she saw a light flash from inside her EVA suit helmet. Where was she? She heard a voice calling her name. *Jann... wake up Jann.*' She opened her eyes and Gizmo was beside her bed. She jumped up and clutched the blanket to her neck.

"So sorry to wake you, Jann, but Nills needs you in the operations room. It appears your colleague Annis has gone walkies."

She arrived to find Nills bent over a 3D map of the Colony One site.

"What's going on?

Nills pointed to a marker on the map. "Annis went EVA

half an hour ago and she's spent the last few minutes inside the MAV."

Jann looked down at the green marker that was First Officer Annis Romanov. How much did she really know about her? Not much, it seemed. Then it started to move out from the MAV, but not back to Colony One. It was heading to the fuel processing plant.

Jann stared at the dot in disbelief.

"How long does it take to prep the MAV?" Nills had a concerned look.

"Around twenty minutes." Then it suddenly dawned on Jann. Annis was getting ready to leave. "Jesus, I don't believe this. She's planning to lift off. Why would she do that?"

"You've got to stop her. We can't let her get back to Earth carrying that bacterium."

Jann looked wide eyed at Nills. "Shit," was all she could manage.

"It would be chaos, if that infection gets loose. Armageddon, the end of human civilization as we know it."

"Shit, shit." The magnitude of the possible devastation that would befall humankind if Annis were to successfully return to Earth was beginning to dawn on her.

"How?"

"Any way you can, you stop her. She must not take off, you've got to stop her."

A nerve shattering scream emanated from just outside the operations room entrance, as the bloodied and broken body of Dr. Paolio Corelli sailed through the doorway and landed with a crash on top of the 3D display. The map flickered off and sparks flew as Paolio's lifeless body buried itself in the remains of the table. Jann turned away from the destruction just in time to see Decker swing a long bar and connect with Nills' extended forearm. He let out a scream and went flying across the operations room floor. Before she could react, Decker pounced on her and swung the bar down hard on her head. She dodged, but it connected with a searing crack on her collarbone. She dropped to the floor as the pain engulfed her. She tumbled backwards and cracked her head on something, blinding her momentarily. When she opened her eyes, Decker was standing over her with the bar held ready to plunge into her chest. But then his whole body started shaking violently. He dropped the bar and it clanged to the floor. Jann grabbed it with her good arm and jumped up. Two long coils of wire ran from prongs embedded in Decker's back to Gizmo's breast panel. A taser. Nills had fitted him with a weapon.

Decker shook. Smoke rose from his body, the skin on his skull blackened and his eyes boiled and hissed in their sockets.

"Gizmo, switch it off." With that Decker stopped shaking and dropped to the floor—dead. Jann turned and staggered over to the forlorn figure of the doctor. "Paolio, I'm so sorry, it's my fault." She touched his bloodied and battered cheek with her hand; tears welled up in her eyes.

"Jann, JANN! You've got to stop her, time is running out." Nills was tugging at her shoulder. "Oh God, Nills, your arm, it's broken."

"It's all right, Gizmo will take care of it... go, go, you've got to go now."

"Okay." She wiped the tears from her eyes, took one last look at Paolio and headed for the airlock. She felt the pain in her shoulder as she donned the EVA suit. It was bad, probably broken. Jann was just about to flip closed the visor when Nills came over. He was holding his arm tight against his body as Gizmo raced behind him with what looked like a syringe. "Nills, be still. I need to give you this for the pain."

"Listen, Jann. You understand what's at stake here. Our lives don't matter. You need to do whatever it is to stop her taking off."

"I know Nills. I know what I have to do now." She reached out and touched his face. "Hey... if... if I don't see you again, it was nice meeting you."

He smiled. "Likewise, it was a pleasure."

The research lab exploded.

SMOKE AND FLAMES burst out from the lab and the force of the blast threw them both across the common room floor. It engulfed them and Jann began to cough and splutter as she tried to orient herself. She looked over at the lab door as a new force hit her. The smoke was being whisked back out into the lab. When it cleared she could see why. There was a black hole where the lab used to be—it was open to the Martian night. Air was being sucked out of the colony at an alarming rate and they were being dragged along with it. Jann slid along the floor with the force of the escaping atmosphere. She grabbed at a table leg and hung on. She could see Gizmo spinning wildly on his back with no apparent control. "Nills, where's Nills?" She saw him sliding past her as he made frantic efforts to grab on to something before he got ejected into the void. She reached out and grabbed him, pulled him in.

Then Jann's EVA suit detected the drop in pressure and automatically closed her visor. "No, no, Nills, no." She looked into his eyes as he struggled to breathe. He clawed at his throat as the oxygen was sucked out of the colony. "No, Nills, goddammit." The force was too strong, she couldn't hold him. He slipped from her grip—and he was gone. Sucked across the floor, through the doorway and out into the Martian night. Jann screamed. She tried to look out through the hole at the far end of the research lab where Nills had been ejected. But the force of the escaping colony atmosphere was such that she was being lifted horizontally off the floor. She clung to the table leg with all her strength to keep from being sucked out.

Nills was gone, Paolio was dead... Decker, Kevin... Lu— all gone. She tried again to look back out through the gap as the facility was being vacuumed clean. She saw Gizmo wedged in an alcove, he didn't seem to be moving. "Even Gizmo is gone," she thought. It was just her now. And Annis, who was now trying to return to Earth, carrying with her the potential destruction of humanity.

HER HAND SLIPPED OFF the table upright, she scrambled to catch it again but the force was too much, she was torn away. Jann rolled and banged her way across the floor, her arms flailing about trying to grab onto anything still screwed down. She bounced off something hard, cartwheeled through the air and slammed into the wall beside the open door to the Research Lab. The air was still rushing through, bringing with it the contents of Colony One. Objects hit off the walls and banged around her head. Jann felt for something to grab onto and found she was pinned against the door of the Research Lab. It was fully open and flat against the wall, held there by the force of the evacuating atmosphere. She inched her way to the outer edge of it, grabbed the inner handle and planted her feet against the wall. She pulled on the handle with all her strength to try and get the door moving. She had it off the wall about two feet when it was hit hard on the side by some heavy flying debris. This added to its momentum, enough for the rush of the air to catch in behind it. She had no time to react. The door swung over with a sudden violence and crashed closed. The shockwave reverberated through the colony superstructure and Jann lost her grip as she was flung across the research lab floor. She spun and slid, then stopped.

She lay there stunned for some time, looking out through the gaping hole in the lab wall, straight at the night sky. All was still and eerily quiet. Slowly Jann sat up and looked around. The lab door was closed and held shut by the inside atmosphere, or what remained of it. She was now effectively outside in the near vacuum of space. She did a quick check of her EVA suit for damage. All looked okay. No warnings, no alerts. She stood up and flipped on her heads up display. Was she too late? Had Annis lifted off? A 3D map illuminated in her field of vision. The markers for the HAB, MAV and the fuel plant hovered over their respective locations. She rotated in their direction. Annis was still on the surface, moving towards the MAV.

She headed for the hole in the Research Lab wall and picked her way through the detritus of the cryo-rack module. It was little more than a shell, split open on all sides. She moved through it, careful not to damage her EVA suit on any of the sharp metal of the walls. At the edge she jumped down onto the surface and swiveled in the direction of the green marker that was First Officer Annis Romanov. She had made her choice, for better or worse she was going to try and save the human race. She ran.

24

MAV

Jann crested the dune and looked out across the Jezero crater. Overhead the nighttime sky sparkled with the light from a universe of suns. Far off in the distant blackness she could just make out lights moving across the planet's surface. It was either one of the rovers or possibly the lights from Annis's EVA helmet. Her first thought when dropping down onto the surface from the wreckage of the research lab, was to switch her own lights on. But she thought better of it as she would rather not announce her arrival. Progress was difficult in the darkness. She wasn't sure of the terrain and had to take it slow so as to not lose her footing. She could tell from the heads-up display that Annis was refueling the MAV. The rover lights correlated with the display markers. She didn't have much time. She moved faster.

Jann hadn't given much thought to how she was going to stop Annis. Perhaps she would just talk to her, try and reason with her. But then again, the first officer had just tried to kill them all and destroy Colony One. And she had achieved pretty much all of that. Only Jann was left. The others were all dead. As for the colony, the damage had to be extensive, possibly even beyond saving.

By now Jann could see the silhouetted figure of the first officer, walking along beside one of the rovers, two large fuel canisters up on top. *How many more did she have to go?* thought Jann. Maybe these were the last. The MAV needed all six to take off. But with only Annis onboard there was a huge weight saving so maybe just four would do. Jann cursed herself for not paying more heed to all the engineering training she had been given. As an astrobiologist she hadn't deemed it necessary. Then again, she never thought she would be in this position. She thought about disabling the MAV in some way, removing some vital part or sticking a proverbial spanner in the works. But again, her lack of engineering knowledge meant she couldn't be sure if what she did would work. Also, it was now becoming clear that Annis would get to the MAV first. In the end the choice was made for her as her EVA suit comms burst into life.

"Jann, I know you're out there. Sorry, but you can't come with me. There's only room for one on this trip."

"Annis, what are you doing?"

"What do you think I'm doing, I'm getting off this contaminated planet."

"Are you crazy? You can't go back, not carrying that infection, it's too dangerous."

"Bullshit."

"No Annis, you have to stop. Annis, for God's sake, listen to me."

"Go screw yourself. You should never have been on this mission in the first place. You never had the smarts for it."

Jann felt a slight tremor underfoot and looked around. Too late. The seismic rover plowed into her at full speed and sent her flying through the air. She landed heavily on the ground and tumbled. That bitch Annis was setting her up all along. Maybe Annis was right; she didn't have the smarts for this. She rolled on the dirt just as the rover drove into her again and rolled over her already damaged left arm. She heard a crack and her body was convulsed by excruciating pain riffling up and across her chest. She screamed.

"Annis, Annis, for God's sake stop." There was no reply. Jann tried to move but the weight was too much. She banged at the rover's paneling with her good arm, but it was pointless. She twisted and squirmed to try and get some movement, but the pain in her side made it impossible.

Suddenly, the robotic arms of the rover sprang to life. Jann tried to fend the grabber away with her right arm but it moved for her throat and pinned her down even more. She banged and pushed. The drill arm started up. "Oh shit." She could see the short drill bit spin furiously as it pointed and moved closer and closer to her helmet visor. She tried to move her head, but it just shifted inside her helmet, which was now firmly held down. The drill tip corkscrewed across her visor as it tried to gain some purchase. It skipped and skated as she frantically banged at it with her free arm. It was now stabbing down, bashing against her faceplate. It didn't need to drill a hole, just a crack would do.

Then Jann saw it, the emergency shutoff panel right above her on the front base of the rover. She raised herself up to flip the cover but struggled to reach. If she could get to it then maybe she'd have a chance. The drill banged down hard and she heard a crack. "Oh shit." Alert lights flashed inside her helmet, to warn her of deteriorating suit integrity. Jann forgot about the pain of her broken bones and frantically pushed with all her strength to flip open the shutoff panel. The rover shifted and slid a little to the left, like one of its wheels had been resting high on some rock, and with her frantic efforts it had slipped off. Her hand reached the panel; she flipped open the cover and punched down on the emergency shutoff. The rover stopped, its drill spun down, its arms lost power.

Jann stopped squirming and she could feel herself breathing hard. She checked the alerts. "Shit." Her faceplate was cracked and she was losing air. The suit tried hard to compensate for the loss in pressure and was using up excessive supplies of nitrogen to rebalance. "Thirty minutes."

She had thirty minutes of air left. Thirty minutes before she died. Thirty minutes to save the world. She laughed. It was an odd feeling. It was not that she was scoffing in the face of death. She was laughing at the absurdity of the situation. The awkward, geeky farm girl. The girl who shouldn't even be here, look at her now. She rolled over and sat up. A stabbing pain shot up her side. "Dammit." She couldn't walk, she would just have to crawl. Jann knew that as soon as Annis realized she had lost remote control of the seismic rover she would be over to finish her off. So she scanned the ground around her, looking for something she could use as a weapon, a sharp rock maybe. But there was nothing obvious to hand. She looked back at the MAV, half expecting to see Annis approaching, but she didn't. Instead she was heading back to the fuel plant with the other rover to get the last of the tanks, presumably having decided that Jann was no longer a threat. And from where Jann was sitting, that would be an accurate assessment of the situation.

She slumped back onto the ground and looked up at the heavens. Above her the vast expanse of the universe was spread out in all its celestial glory, as if to mock the insignificance of her very existence. What could she do? Maybe it was better to let Annis go. Maybe the decimation of the human race would be the best thing for the planet. A cull of a species that was destroying their own home. Too many, too greedy, too stupid... or just simply too successful.

She could hop or maybe crawl back to the HAB in the

time left to her. "Twenty-three minutes." She could save herself... maybe, if she went now. It would be cutting it fine, even with that. She sat up again and tried to stand. The pain in her leg was excruciating now that the initial rush of adrenaline had worn off. She reached over and pulled herself up using the deactivated seismic rover for help. She stood there for a minute, gathering the remains of her strength, trying not to breathe too much. She rested her head in her arms on the top of the rover and looked down along its side. The bright ISA logo seemed to fluoresce in the Martian night. She stopped, and looked again. Beside the logo, on the door of a storage compartment on the side of the rover, were marked the words *caution, seismic charges*. Jann looked at it for a minute as an idea began to formulate in her mind. "Twenty-one minutes." Up ahead, Annis was still en route to the fuel dump.

Jann sat back down again so she could get better access to the rover's storage compartment. She flipped open the door, reached in and took out a charge. They could be detonated remotely; she just needed to tag the charge to her control. She held it in her hand for a moment and contemplated the consequences of what she was planning. Being able to detonate it meant nothing unless she could get the rover to the MAV, or the fuel dump. Or should she just kill Annis? "Twenty minutes." It also meant she would not be able to reach the HAB before the oxygen in her suit dropped to a point where she would lose consciousness and die. She looked over again at Annis. In the darkness she could see the beams of light from her helmet bob along the Martian surface towards the fuel dump. If she was going to do this she needed to do it now. It would mean her own death but, as Nills had said, what did that matter against the enormity of the devastation that would be wrought if this bacterium made it to Earth?

She flipped the cap on the charge and tagged it to her control. She set it back in its compartment along with all the others and closed the door. She then crawled around to the back of the rover where the control panel was and switched it on. The screen illuminated, displaying options for rover operation. Jann deactivated all remote control functionality so that Annis could not hijack it again. She then tagged it to Annis' suit. Now, as soon as she switched the power on again, the rover would dutifully roll off to rendezvous with the first officer. It was now or never. Jann hit the power button and moved back. The rover took a few seconds to orient itself, read its new instruction set, and then it moved off to find Annis. "Nineteen minutes."

The first officer had reached the fuel plant and was loading up the last of the canisters. She stopped when she noticed the seismic rover moving in her direction.

"Jann, are you still alive out there?"

It was Jann's turn not to reply.

"What are you trying to do, run me over? Well, that's pathetic. But then again you always were a total waste of space."

She could hear Annis laugh at her own joke.

"Too late anyway, it's time to go."

Annis hefted the last canister and started off. The seismic rover noticed the change in direction and turned to follow. "Twelve minutes." The rover closed the gap, Jann flipped on her 3D control interface.

"I'm sorry Annis, but you leave me no choice." She hit detonate.

AN EXPLOSION in the thin atmosphere of Mars is a strange phenomenon. There's virtually no sound. It was just a slight tremor that Jann felt as the nighttime sky illuminated in a fiery ball of methane/oxygen rocket fuel. The light was blinding and she covered her visor with her arm and looked away. There was a brief moment before the debris rained down, peppering the entire area with dust and rocks and shards of metal. It was some time before Jann ventured to look again after the last of the destruction had stopped falling. She couldn't see much, just an enormous plume of dust. She switched on her helmet lights but even they could not penetrate the murky darkness. She switched them off and rolled onto her back. *Nine minutes, well this is it,* she thought. Now it was time to die. She had prevented the decimation of human civilization and no one would know, no one would care. It was her time now, her work was done.

The EVA suit blinked a new alert to warn its occupant of

the impending low oxygen emergency. From her training, she knew it would now try to maximize the remaining reserves by substituting nitrogen. This way her body would still feel like it was breathing, even though there would be less and less oxygen in each breath. It was a calm way to die; she would simply drift into unconsciousness and never wake up.

"Five minutes."

As her mind drifted, she had the feeling of being lifted up towards the canopy of twinkling stars. They began to move, *or was it her that was moving*, like she was being transported somewhere. She felt no fear, no pain and no care. Her eyes closed and she drifted off into the heavens.

25

THE GARDEN

The sudden loss of atmosphere from Colony One could have been the end of the facility, save for the fact that Jann had managed to close the lab's inner door while she was being ejected. By this action she had averted a potential catastrophe. As soon as the tsunami of evacuating air had ceased, Gizmo was able to right itself and could now move into action. Since there were no longer any Earthlings in the colony it could get radical with the analysis of priorities. It shut down unnecessary sectors and killed power to all nonessential systems. It set about rerouting energy and reassigning all priority protocols to the biodome, trying to bring it back up to nominal levels and stabilize the fragile ecosystem. After monitoring the effects of its efforts it estimated it could save 67.3% of biomass and 71.2% of diversity. It meant that several plant species had now become extinct on Mars. However, this would still depend on it physically fixing the damaged infrastructure within the biodome. So it raced around righting hydroponics, untangling ducting and covering exposed root systems.

It was during these latter tasks that a new data stream entered its silicon consciousness. It was another life support system going critical. But this was not in Colony One, this was out on the planet's surface. At some point Nills had interfaced Dr. Jann Malbec's EVA suit with colony systems so that he, and Gizmo, would get feedback on her state. Gizmo considered its own internal instruction set for any preprogrammed routines that were to be executed for such an event and found none. However, after it ascertained that it had no preset actions to take, it did the next thing on its list of priorities—Gizmo analyzed the situation.

Its number one priority had always been to ensure the safety of Nills Langthorp, but he was now dead, blown out through the hole in the Research Lab wall. It also assessed that no other human was alive on the surface of Mars, save for ISA crewmember Dr. Jann Malbec, whose life was fading fast. But, it was precedence that tipped the balance for Gizmo. Nills had saved her life before, back when the demented commander tried to kill her in the Medlab. So this must have been a priority for Nills and therefore, by extension, for Gizmo. The final decider was its analysis that it had a 54.8% probability of saving her life. All this, its silicon mind calculated, in a fraction of a microsecond.

Gizmo made its way to a functioning airlock and exited out onto the planet's surface. Its tracked wheels enabled it to race across the dusty terrain at great speed. By the time it found her and lifted her up she was just losing consciousness. Gizmo finally got her back through the airlock just as the EVA suit shut down.

It took the little robot several attempts to resuscitate her on the medlab operating table, but on the fourth attempt Jann's body responded and she sucked in a long gulp of air. She was still unconscious while Gizmo tended to her broken bones, and it was several hours later before she opened her eyes, looked around, and spoke.

"Gizmo, how did I get here?"

"I brought you here."

"I thought I died."

"Well, technically you did, I rebooted you."

She looked at the quirky machine for a moment. "Thank you, Gizmo."

"Don't mention it, the pleasure is all mine."

BUT THAT WAS a long time ago now and many months had passed. The colony's systems now hummed and sung with optimal perfection and the biodome had regained much of its lush verdant abundance. Yet it was different. A new wildness had taken over. More tropical forest than kitchen garden. Gizmo whizzed through the connecting tunnel and into the biodome. It zipped along the racks of hydroponics until it came to the edge of the forest area near the center of the vast dome. It slowed down so as not to cause damage to the velvety carpet that was the forest floor, a thick mat of mosses and grasses. It was a product of diligent bioengineering, hard work and time. It moved through the worn gap in the tall overgrown vegetation and out onto the central dais. The pond shimmered and the splash from the tall rock waterfall prismed the morning light into a myriad of twinkling colors.

Standing at the base of the waterfall, Dr. Jann Malbec held her head back as she washed her hair in the gently falling cascade. Gizmo watched from the edge of the pond and waited patiently. She stepped out, shook the excess water from her hair and waded across the pond, carp scattering as she went. She spotted Gizmo.

"Ah... good morning."

"Good morning Jann, I trust you had a good sleep."

"I did, Gizmo, thank you."

"I have brought you some breakfast. It's the last of the coffee, I'm afraid."

"Not to worry, I think there's some still left in the HAB. Next time we're outside we can bring back the remaining supplies." She bit into some toast and sipped her coffee. She was naked. Over the last few months Jann had found herself with little reason to get dressed. With no humans for more than 140 million miles there were a lot of things that don't seem so important anymore. Putting on clothes was one of them.

It took only four weeks for her bones to heal enough for her to use her arm again. A remarkably speedy recovery. During that time she had learned as much as she could from Gizmo on the state of the colony after the research lab explosion. Between them, they nursed it back to health and sustainability. It was another few weeks more before she finally ventured out on the surface again and made her way to the HAB. She found the COM communications unit and realized the extent of the first officer's deceit. They brought it back to Colony One, along with the satellite unit, and Gizmo reconfigured it to function for ISA transmission protocols. So, it was over two months before Jann sent a long report back to mission control.

It had been assumed on Earth that the colony was destroyed and all crew lost. With no communication all they had to go on was the satellite data. It showed images of the destruction at the colony and also the catastrophic loss of the fuel plant. The MAV was still intact, but with no fuel to power it, it was useless. Jann was stuck on Mars, there was no way to return to Earth, unless a new fuel manufacturing plant could be built and new canisters fashioned. Mission control sent her detailed plans on how to do this with materials available in the colony, but she was not great at engineering and, in truth, she was in no hurry to return. The next launch window was not for another year and a half, anyway. She was also beginning to fall under the same spell that Nills had talked about, and as the weeks went by she became more and more at one—with Colony One.

She replaced the hammock that Nills had used with a low futon and curled up on it at night, looking out through the dome at the infinite universe. During these nights she began to gain a deeper understanding of what it meant to be human. It was a kind of feral reawakening. A sense of wild abandon bubbled up inside her and she began to understand how Nills must have felt. And, like him, she realized the critical importance of Gizmo for maintaining her sanity. The human mind was a fragile thing, kept in balance only by the company of others. We are social animals, we feel safe in the herd, and desire its acceptance. Alone, the human mind wanders with no clear purpose, nothing to keep it in balance.

"WILL you be requiring clothing today, Jann?"

Jann thought about this a moment. Clothing did have one big advantage in the colony—pockets. Her daily dressing considerations had effectively been reduced to whether pockets would be useful in performing whatever tasks she had assigned for herself that day.

"Or would you prefer more time to think about it?"

"Yes, there's no rush, we can decide later." She sipped her coffee and sat down on a low chair to dry her hair.

"Tell me Gizmo, do you miss Nills?"

"Alas, poor Nills, I knew him well. A man of infinite jest."

"That sounds like Shakespeare."

"That's because it is. From Hamlet."

Jann laughed and sipped her coffee. "You have no concept of death Gizmo, do you?"

"I understand it is reality for living entities. I understand that Nills no longer exists."

Jann put the towel down and lay back on the recliner like she was sunning herself by the pool. "That's not, strictly speaking, true."

"You mean he's still alive?"

"In a sense."

"Explain. I hate to admit it, but I am confused."

"Remember when we checked the MAV and we found one of the analogues from the bio-rack in the research lab? Annis was trying to return to Earth with it."

"I do. Curious, that."

"Well here's the thing, I finally managed to cross reference it with data I had gleaned from the lab IT systems before it was destroyed, and guess what?"

"It's Nills."

"Correct. So in a sense, part of him still exists. Even if it *is* just a facsimile."

"The plot thickens."

"Indeed it does, Gizmo. For one, why did COM want

Annis to bring this back to Earth? And second, what was it about Nills that was so special?"

"Again, I have to admit I have no answer."

Jann sat up on the recliner and looked directly at Gizmo. "Did you ever notice any physiological changes in Nills over the time you were together?"

"Sure. Beard, no beard. Clothed, naked. Clean, not clean. There were many."

"No, I mean more subtle than that."

"Now that you mention it, I did notice that my recognition algorithm was losing accuracy by approximately 12.34% per year. This I attributed to aging and compensated for it accordingly."

"Well, as always Gizmo, you are correct. But he was not getting older. No, he was getting younger."

"My understanding is that is not possible."

"It's not probable. But in this instance, it would seem that it is indeed possible."

"Holy cow."

Jann laughed at the little robot and stood up.

"So what happens now, Jann?"

"What do you think?"

The little robot paused for a beat and then replied. "They will come for it. If they wanted it that badly, they will return here to get it."

"My thinking exactly. But that can't be for at least another year and a half."

"So we have some time."

"We do. And time that I need to find out exactly what was going on here. My guess is that COM were on the cusp of some major genetic breakthrough. They may have even achieved it. But all was lost when the sandstorm hit and the infection broke out. I intend to find out what it was that they were doing."

"Is that possible with the research lab destroyed?"

"Doubtful. That's why I think we'll need to investigate the mine at some point. I would really like to know what was going on over there."

"When do we start?"

"Oh… there's no rush, Gizmo. Time enough for that." She looked around at the vast biodome. "Anyway, I don't really want to leave. I'm beginning to like it here too much."

TO BE CONTINUED...

ALSO BY GERALD M. KILBY

Why not check out the next book in the series, Colony Two Mars.

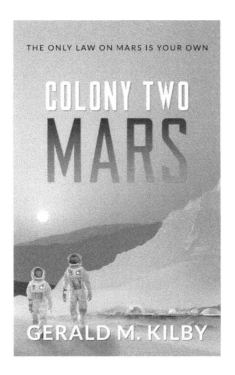

The only survivor of the ill-fated ISA mission is now stranded on Mars. Having been designated a bio-hazard by Earth, any hope of returning home is all but gone. She is abandoned, isolated, and alone.

ABOUT THE AUTHOR

Gerald M. Kilby grew up on a diet of Isaac Asimov, Arthur C. Clark, and Frank Herbert, which developed into a taste for Iain M. Banks and everything ever written by Neal Stephenson. Understandable then, that he should choose science fiction as his weapon of choice when entering the fray of storytelling.

REACTION is his first novel and is very much in the old-school techno-thriller style and you can get it free here. His latest books, **COLONY MARS** and **THE BELT,** are both best sellers, topping Amazon charts for Hard Science Fiction and Space Exploration. Colony Mars has also been optioned by **Hollywood for a potential new TV series.**

He lives in the city of Dublin, Ireland, in the same neighborhood as Bram Stoker and can be sometimes seen tapping away on a laptop in the local cafe with his dog Loki.

You can connect with Gerald M. Kilby at:
www.geraldmkilby.com

Milton Keynes UK
Ingram Content Group UK Ltd.
UKHW020927271223
434976UK00015B/648